DAY

✓ Manicure and pedicure
✓ Haircut

DAY TWO—The outfits
✓ Five dresses, one for each day of Pierce Stanton's show

DAY THREE—Interview Valerie, or "Who am I?"
✓ Why she writes the novels she does
✓ How she feels about her millions of fans

DAY FOUR—Tie up my life (what little there is of it)
✓ Phone my agent
✓ Ask Al to feed Chaplin and collect mail

DAY FIVE—More shopping with Valerie
✓ Lingerie
✓ *Shoes!!!*

DAY SIX—Relax!
✓ Read advance copy of Valerie's newest novel

DAY SEVEN—A day with Mom

DAY EIGHT—The adventure begins!
✓ Fly nonstop from New York to Chicago—and Pierce Stanton

Piece of cake!

Dear Reader,

I was thrilled to learn that Harlequin Books was rereleasing *Another Chance at Heaven*. Family relationships, especially the complex bonds between sisters, have always fascinated me.

I have an older sister, as Genie does, but she is nothing like Valerie. We're twenty-two months apart and could pass for twins. When people meet us, they stare at first one, then the other. We've played tricks on our friends, though the farthest I've ever gone was impersonating my sister over the phone. (Yes, we *sound* exactly alike, too!)

Though siblings may have their ups and downs, there is no one on earth who understands a woman like her sister. They share family history, and they've been through so much with each other. The strangest part of the journey is how two women usually go from bickering childhood rivals to the closest and dearest of friends.

I didn't dedicate this novel to anyone when it first came out, but I think I wrote it with my sister in mind. So, Avis, this one's for you! And I hope all of you have as much fun with Genie and Valerie's story as I did.

All my best in romantic reading,

Elda Minger

ELDA MINGER

Another Chance at Heaven

HARLEQUIN®

TORONTO • NEW YORK • LONDON
AMSTERDAM • PARIS • SYDNEY • HAMBURG
STOCKHOLM • ATHENS • TOKYO • MILAN • MADRID
PRAGUE • WARSAW • BUDAPEST • AUCKLAND

ISBN-13: 978-0-373-36134-2
ISBN-10: 0-373-36134-3

ANOTHER CHANCE AT HEAVEN

This edition published by arrangement with Harlequin Books S.A.

www.eHarlequin.com

Printed in U.S.A.

ELDA MINGER

is a bestselling, award-winning and versatile author of dozens of romance novels, including series, contemporary and historical. She is also known for her informative and entertaining workshops on writing. Elda lives in California with her family, both two- and four-footed.

Chapter One

"My honest opinion?" Genie looked her older sister, Valerie, straight in the eye. "It's the stupidest idea I've ever heard."

"Geneviève!" Valerie Bouchet waved her elegantly manicured fingertips in the air, then clasped them together and leaned forward so her face was inches away from Genie's. "You have to help me. I have to let my publicist know soon."

Genie sighed. So like Valerie to be so ditzy, never taking anyone else's plans into consideration. How had she let her sister talk her into this farce of a lunch?

Old habits die hard. Ever since she could remember, Valerie had been the flaky one in the family, she the rock. "Oh, Valerie can't help it—that's just the way she is" had become something of a family refrain. Genie had always felt she lived her life in her sister's shadow, for to look at Valerie was to be dazzled. Like staring too long at the sun. Utterly beautiful and sure of herself, Valerie had always made Genie feel reduced to clumsiness, like a long-limbed adolescent.

There were other reasons as well. *My traitorous stomach.* Genie could clearly visualize the Spartan kitchen in her apartment on Ninety-second Street. One could eat only macaroni and cheese for so long. But studying the crab quiche on the china plate in front of her, she found she didn't have any appetite.

Genie lowered her voice. "Valerie, the women who read your books *adore* you. They're not going to be upset to learn you're thirty-seven years old."

Her sister's hands fluttered nervously to her rounded stomach. In the final stages of her pregnancy, Valerie looked better than any woman had the right to. Her long dark hair was lustrous, and the sharp lines of her face had softened. Genie knew her sister was anxious about this baby. She had miscarried two years ago. This pregnancy was very important to her.

"You don't understand," Valerie said, her voice agitated. "I want them to see me as I'd like to be—as they'd *want* me to be! I'm absolutely hideous! You look exactly like I did when I was younger. With some skillful makeup, no one will be any wiser."

Genie sighed. It was too bad Valerie couldn't take their mother as an example. Madame Bouchet lived her life with such grace; her facial lines and gray hair gave her added character. A woman who embraced life with passion, she had tried to teach both her daughters that looks were secondary to so many other qualities and a woman grew infinitely more interesting with age.

She failed so miserably with Val. But her sister's next words brought Genie back to the present problem.

"Anyway, what do you have to do that's so all-important? Your acting career is going nowhere. You live in that horrible little apartment. You never look like you've had enough to eat, Maman worries constantly about you—"

"Enough, Val." She was surprised when her sister stopped talking. So unlike her. Genie sighed as she carefully laid her fork on the china plate and lifted a glass of Pouilly Fouissé to her lips. Lunch in a restaurant like this, one of New York City's finest, was enough to wipe out her weekly budget. But Valerie took it all in stride, whipping out her gold credit card, not even glancing at the bill.

To have money like that. To not worry constantly. Genie shook her head slightly. She'd made her choice in life.

"Can I call you tonight?" Valerie asked almost an hour later as they walked outside into the pale winter sunlight.

Something just wasn't right about this. Genie felt frustrated by the entire conversation. "After eleven. I'm going to a movie with Al."

Valerie wrinkled her nose in disgust. Al was not one of her favorite people. "I'll be up, then. Be sure to pick up if I call. I don't want to hear that damned message again." She stepped off the curb and tried to hail a taxi, looking magnificent though bulky in her black cape and boots. As Genie watched her sister, she detected a look of desperation on her face. Why was this whole situation so crucial to her?

Before she stepped inside the yellow cab that had shot up next to the curb, Valerie tried to convince her one last time. "Please, Genie. Consider it, won't you?"

Despite her misgivings, Genie put a reassuring hand on her sister's arm. Strange that though she was ten years younger than Val, she'd always felt protective of her. "I will. I'll let you know by the end of the week."

"WONDERFUL INTERVIEW, Pierce."

"You were magnificent!"

"You brought out facets I never thought she possessed."

As Pierce Stanton answered each comment with a slight smile and a polite reply, he glanced at the clock. Only a few minutes more. Then he could leave, go home, shed his public persona like a lizard shedding its skin.

He stepped inside his office as soon as he could, shutting the door behind him to ensure his privacy. Tension deemed to drain out of his body. No longer in the public eye, he could let down his instinctive guard.

When had he stopped enjoying his work? When he had begun to ask questions because they were on the master sheet and not because he was truly interested in what his guest had to say?

You're burning out. At only thirty-three. Wearily, he put a hand to the back of his neck and massaged the slowly loosening muscles. He felt as if he were dying inside.

A change. You need a change. But even as he thought the words, he knew he would finish out his contract. Just until Christmas. He could generate enough energy to justify his considerable salary. It was the right thing to do.

Especially if Valerie Bouchet agreed to be interviewed.

He walked over to his leather chair behind the massive oak desk and sat down. Before he leaned back, he picked up the hardcover book his secretary Anne had placed on his desk earlier that day.

Valerie. Ever since the whole unbelievably messy

incident with his sister, Barbara, and her husband, he'd been keeping an eye on her. Waiting. Confident their paths would cross sooner or later. The moment he'd been anticipating for almost five years would be arriving soon. And he doubted she knew he was waiting for her.

In his mind's eye, he could see Barbara's pale, anguished face as she told him about her husband's infidelity. Robert had flaunted Valerie in her face, like an immature child with a new toy. Pierce had listened to her, understanding her pain. It had brought back so much of his own. His contempt for Valerie Bouchet had begun to grow on that hot summer night, years ago.

He'd read all her books. She was a damn good writer, with uncanny insight into the fast-paced lives of rich and famous people who used others like pawns in their personal chess games. And Pierce classed Valerie right in with the people she wrote about.

If one believed publicity, Valerie's life sounded like a modern-day fairy tale. From a poor background she had married money in the form of Harold Jameson, producer. Her husband had introduced her to the world she wrote about, and their tumultuous relationship had been major news. They had lived together for seven years before they married. Valerie had an uncanny way of soaking up her surroundings, and she'd put to good advantage the new world she began to move around in when she met Harold. Her first three books had been instant bestsellers, exposing the way life in the fastest lane of all was explored to its fullest. But lately, all news of Valerie centered around the sudden changes in her life, her desire to be the devoted wife and partner. Pierce suspected it was another clever facade.

And what a facade it was. He studied the photo on the back of the book jacket. *Valerie.* Everyone's fantasy. Sensual. Wanton. Her waist-length blue-black hair spilled over her bare shoulders. Her eyes, the color of strong tea, smoldered, promised the camera so many things Pierce knew she did her best to deliver in private. How could any suburban housewife hope to compete with a woman who depicted torridly sensual love affairs—and looked like the women she wrote about?

Pierce studied the picture for a long time in the solitude of his office. He had to admit he could see how she'd make a man's blood catch fire. The ruby-red gown was cut deeply enough to reveal firm, full breasts. The gown fit tightly over her small waist and curved hips. Her legs were long and slender, her feet perfect in their delicate leather high-heeled shoes. A diamond-and-ruby necklace adorned her throat, and matching jewelry graced her ears and fingers.

But it was all in her eyes. Their expression compelled a man to drown himself in their sensual depths. Large, thickly fringed with black spiky lashes, they provided a startling contrast against her white skin.

She was exquisite. What made Valerie Bouchet unusual was that although she wrote about millions of women's erotic fantasies, she fulfilled many a man's. Visually, at least.

He was going to prepare for her appearance. He knew she'd come. The publicity value of his show was too good to turn down. And Valerie wasn't stupid. During the week he'd have her on his talk show, he'd make her realize the harm she'd inflicted on his sister.

Strange, now that the moment had come, he felt no uneasiness about what he was planning to do—humiliate a media star on national television. His show had the power to make or break an author.

And he intended to break through her façade. He'd make her look like the woman he knew her to be. It was something he had promised himself on that hot August night many years ago.

He owed Barbara that much.

"SHE WANTS you to do *what?*" Al asked, his hazel eyes full of amusement. They had decided against the movie and instead were sharing a pizza in her kitchen.

"She has a new book coming out," Genie explained. "Her publicist arranged for her to do Pierce Stanton's talk show in Chicago. But she wants me to go."

"She wants you to impersonate her?" Al sounded incredulous as he bit into a piece of pizza. It had a thick crust and was topped with everything imaginable. Genie had also bought an inexpensive bottle of burgundy, and they were seated around the butcher block Valerie had given her last Christmas.

Genie nodded. "She's terrified at the thought of growing old. She looks terrific to me—all she does is run from salon to salon."

"And write her books," Al mused. "I read the last one. She's a hell of a good writer."

"She's also scared about the baby. I wish she'd just cancel the whole thing until after her pregnancy is over. I'm worried about her."

"But it's not only the baby that's bothering you," Al said, encouraging her to continue speaking out her thoughts.

"There's something here that doesn't click." Genie poured Al more wine, then settled back into her chair. Chaplin, a small black mutt Genie had rescued while he was scrounging through the garbage last winter, looked up at her from underneath her chair, his brown eyes begging her for a tidbit. She pulled a piece of sausage off the pizza and tossed it to him. He caught it quickly, then wagged his tail and gave her a doggy smile.

They ate in silence, enjoying a friendship spanning almost four years. Genie had met Al at the corner deli on her second day in the city. Al, as adept as Genie at picking up strays, had recognized her fear and confusion. New York City was nothing like the small town out on Long Island Genie had grown up in.

And she had recognized in Al, underneath his cocky bravado, a twenty-year-old man who was scared to death and needed someone to listen to his fears . Although Al was three years younger than she was, Genie was constantly amazed by the depth of his perception when it came to people. It was what made him such a sensitive friend, such a fine actor.

And both of them knew what a step it had been to come to Manhattan. Al, born in Brooklyn, had lived in the shadow of the city all his life. He'd been determined to escape the fate his older brothers had been handed, working in their father's corner grocery. A member of a large, overpowering Italian family, he'd learned independence quickly and kept his dreams to himself. Once he'd gotten to know Genie, she told him about her struggle to find the courage to leave her hometown. He had understood immediately.

She was so lucky to have Al as a friend. He'd been the one to help her through the maze of pictures, résumés, classes, "go sees," theater bookstores, unions—and now, this job with Val. At twenty-seven, Genie had yet to set the world on fire. But it wasn't for lack of trying.

Al put down his fork, then peeled off a piece of pepperoni for Chaplin, tossing it underneath the table. "Okay. You want to know my biggest nightmare?"

She nodded, wondering what could possibly frighten Al. He always seemed so confident.

"I think about being doomed to take the part of Nicely Nicely in *Guys and Dolls* on the dinner theater circuit for the rest of my life."

To an actor, being doomed to dinner theater for the rest of his life was a fate worse than death. Nothing proclaimed more succinctly he just hadn't made it. It was almost better simply to change professions and admit defeat.

And Al was twenty-four, of medium height, with dark thinning hair and a roly-poly figure. The consummate character actor. It hurt him professionally that because his looks didn't scream beefcake, he wasn't considered for many younger leading-man roles. These days, whatever part he was offered, he took. A job was a job.

"So," Al said, looking at her intently, "there's a hell of a lot to be said for taking opportunities when they come to you."

Genie ate the last bite of her slice, then wiped her hands on a paper towel before reaching for her glass of wine. "I think you're right."

"You sound real confident."

"I don't know. It's just something I saw in her eyes this afternoon—"

"How much is she paying you for your time?"

Genie quoted a figure that made Al raise his eyebrows and whistle softly. "You could buy a lot of time with money like that. Not to mention pictures and résumés."

"I know, but—"

"Genie, get practical. It's a job, plain and simple."

"Do you want any more of this?" she asked, indicating the pizza carton.

"Don't change the subject. Think of how this could help your career. No more waitressing—"

"Al—"

"No more burns on your arms from the hot trays, no more sore feet. Plenty of energy for auditions. Speaking of which, you'd better get to bed if you want to be on top of things tomorrow."

"Yes, mother." She grinned at him. "Thanks, Al. It helps me sort my feelings out just to talk."

He picked up his jacket from the back of the chair. "Just approach it like a role. Read Valerie's books. Talk to her about writing. Research it the way you'd research any other part. You're a whiz with makeup—no one will be any wiser. Now let me out and get to bed. You're going to need all your energy for your audition tomorrow."

"HONEY, IT'S ALL OVER," the actress next to her whispered.

"What?" Genie was sure she'd heard her incorrectly.

"Look who the producer just brought in."

Genie glanced over to the far side of the theater. The producer, a short, balding man, had a young blonde on his arm. Her bodily proportions were stunning. Bending his head, he whispered something in her ear. The petite woman giggled, then put a hand over her mouth.

"Pack it up," the actress whispered to Genie. "Better luck next time, kid."

"But I haven't even read yet," Genie whispered.

"How long have you been in the business, honey? You'd better toughen up. When I tell you it's over, it's over."

As Genie continued to stare at the blonde, the actress said softly, "I've seen it a thousand times, and it still makes me sick. They ask the impossible—stay open enough emotionally to be creative and put up with this shit at the same time. Wait and see—I know I'm right about this."

You'd better toughen up. Genie played the older actress's words over in her head as she walked briskly toward the subway. She'd taken a cab to the theatre for confidence, but finances dictated the subway home. Burying her hands deeper in the pockets of her down coat, she lowered her chin against the bitterly cold wind.

Toughen up. As if it were possible by just saying the words. The reality of the business was a hard concept to come to terms with. Genie had seen so much of it in her classes—the older actors, men and women, still living in their cheap singles eating off their hot plates, waiting for their "big break." She had sworn to herself—at the age of twenty-three when she'd started taking herself seriously as an aspiring actress, she would never end up like them.

The subway ride seemed to last forever. But soon she was back above ground, walking briskly to keep warm. When she opened the door to the restaurant she worked at, the warm air hit her in the face, and it seemed to Genie she was suffocating.

Inside the bathroom, she quickly donned her uniform, a black minidress and white frilly apron.

I'M GOING TO DO IT.

Genie took the steps to her third-floor apartment slowly. Her feet ached from doing a double-duty shift, both the lunch and dinner crowd, with only one quick break between. Her head ached from the noise. Her butt ached from three pinches at the bar.

Once at her door, she opened it slowly. She threw her mail on the small table by the couch, not wanting to open it. The phone bill. The gas bill. Nothing new, nothing good. The same old stuff.

Toward the end of her shift, Genie had taken a good long look at the direction her life was taking. Not a patient person by nature, and having had an absolutely horrible evening, she'd made her decision when a customer had started complaining about the toughness of his steak. It seemed to Genie if she heard one more person complain, took one more order, did one more thing she didn't want to do, she'd go absolutely crazy.

So take the job. See Chicago. You'll be doing Val a favor and helping yourself at the same time. Just get out of the rut you're in. It was an impulsive, purely emotional decision, and Genie decided to go with it. Sitting down on the couch, she kicked off her heels, dialing Valerie's number at the same time. Her sister picked up on the second ring.

"Val? I'll do it." Genie tried to make herself sound cheerful. After all, it was only a job. One week of her life. Perhaps her instincts about Valerie's feelings were completely wrong.

"Darling, that's *wonderful!* Can you meet me for breakfast tomorrow? We have so much planning to do...."

THE NEXT FEW DAYS were a total whirl for Genie. Valerie took her all over Manhattan. The first day she was massaged, masked, manicured, pedicured, steamed, wrapped, scented and smoothed. Her hair was shampooed, trimmed, conditioned and styled. Her legs were waxed. There wasn't one inch of her that wasn't gone over in transforming her into Valerie Bouchet, bestselling author *extraordinaire.*

The next day they shopped. Valerie picked out clothes, and Genie tried them on. Five dresses, one for each day she was to be on Pierce Stanton's show. Valerie took her to private showrooms, where her favorite designers had made up stunning creations to reflect Valerie's stunning personality. Though Genie wore the same size as Valerie, her figure was slimmer.

"It's a little low, don't you think?" Genie asked as she stared down at the deep-veed neckline of a drop-dead little black number. She could easily imagine her sister draping this slip of a dress over her body. Genie preferred her well-worn jeans, sweatshirts and leotards.

"It's perfect. You have to wear a strapless bra with it, something with a little push, you know?"

"But I'll fall out!" Genie was horrified, picturing herself exposed on nationwide television.

Valerie smiled indulgently. "Glue yourself in."

Genie sighed. "Val, is all this really necessary?"

Her sister raised a finely arched eyebrow. "Genie, you must *feel* sensual in every part of your body. My image is that of a seductive woman. It's all part of getting into character, isn't it? Didn't you learn that in your classes? You should realize just what it is I'm trying to do with you.''

Resigned, Genie stared at herself in the mirror. She'd need more than this dress to think of herself as a sensual woman. Maybe with the right makeup and new shoes....

The third day was spent talking with her sister about Val's career. How it had started, why she wrote what she did, how she felt about the millions of women who read her books. Valerie was a stern taskmaster, and Genie felt prepared to answer any question Pierce or the audience might throw at her. She was touched by the insight she received into her sister's personality. It seemed Valerie lived her life through her books, her involvement was that intense. She had shut herself away from the rest of the world and had a reputation as the Garbo of the publishing industry. There was absolutely nothing she did but write, other than attend to her husband, Harold, and her poodle, Miel. In her earlier days, before she'd settled down, she partied away every night. Now she simply concentrated on becoming a better writer, making each book more satisfying than the last.

The fourth day, Genie spent tying up her life. She phoned her agent and left a message saying she'd be in Chicago for a week but promised to call her again with a number where she could be reached. Impulsively, she quit her job, and Al was going to house-sit her apartment, feed Chaplin and collect her mail.

She went shopping with Valerie again on the fifth day. This time Val bought her silk lingerie, incredibly supple leather shoes and accessories for her five outfits. Genie picked out the makeup necessary for her transformation, and they spent the evening at Valerie's penthouse apartment experimenting with different looks until Valerie was satisfied.

"Now," she instructed, her voice firm, "no matter what the weather is like in Chicago, insist they send a limousine for you every morning. You must get to the studio in one piece."

Genie knew her sister was satisfied with their creation. Valerie pulled her designer luggage out of a closet and helped Genie pack, carefully folding sheets of tissue around the expensive clothing. The scent of leather and fine fabrics filled the bedroom as she expertly arranged Genie's clothing. Makeup went in a separate bag, to be carried on the plane. Valerie left nothing to chance, and Genie was beginning to realize why her sister was so successful.

"You'll spend the night before your flight here, and Harold will drive you to the airport. The minute you step out that door Sunday morning, you'll be me. Do you understand?"

Genie nodded, impressed. Valerie had thought of every detail. It was strange, because usually she was such a ditz. Yet something still seemed to be worrying her sister. It was in the depths of her eyes, at moments when Genie was positive Valerie wasn't aware she was watching her. But nothing Genie could put a finger to. Perhaps she was worried about her baby.

The last thing Valerie did was give Genie an advance copy of her newest novel. She called a taxi and walked her sister downstairs to the lobby.

"You might want to catch the show on television. Pierce Stanton is supposed to be an excellent interviewer. It wouldn't hurt to know what you're up against."

Her sister's word choice was revealing. "What do you mean, up against?"

Valerie played with a strand of her dark hair nervously. "Genie, I've never enjoyed giving interviews—they upset me. And you know my doctor doesn't want me upset now." As she spoke Valerie gently put her hands over her protruding stomach. "I haven't given many in my career because I've always been afraid." She paused for a fraction of a second. "You're the actress in the family."

GENIE SPENT FRIDAY relaxing and reading Valerie's novel. Saturday she visited her mother out on Long Island. And Sunday morning, after kissing Harold goodbye in the VIP lounge at Kennedy Airport, Genie-Valerie Bouchet stepped on a nonstop flight headed for Chicago.

And Pierce Stanton.

Chapter Two

Genie picked up the telephone softly buzzing in her hotel suite, removed a diamond earring, and put the receiver to her ear.

"Hello?" She consciously pitched her voice so it came out low and husky. Sensual.

"Ms. Bouchet?"

"Yes." And she was. Genie had spent the better part of the morning getting into character. As each sheer layer of clothing and makeup was skillfully applied, she'd become Valerie Bouchet.

"The limousine is waiting downstairs."

"Thank you. I'll be right down."

As she hung up the phone, she refastened the earring securely, then picked up her bag and fur cape and turned to look in the large mirror over the dresser.

Perfect. The strapless scarlet silk dress hugged her hips just enough. She had left her long black waist-length hair loose, as her sister had instructed her. Valerie had even given her a wedding band.

Her makeup was flawless, the dark plum blusher emphasizing her high cheekbones, the smoky-blue shadow defining her large eyes, huge in her pale face.

Her nails, her leather heels, even her silk underwear—perfection.

Making sure she had her hotel key with her, she left the suite. After all, she thought, with a quick grin that was pure Genie, Valerie Bouchet was not the sort of woman who locked herself out of a hotel room.

It was bitterly cold. Gusts of wind came slicing up off the canopy surface of Lake Michigan. But Genie was only exposed to the raw weather for mere seconds, then ushered inside a luxurious limousine. As she snuggled beneath a fur throw, she thought of the grimy subways she rode every day in New York. But now she was Valerie.

The limousine pulled smoothly away from the curb and headed toward the studio. Genie looked out the window, anxious to take in a new city. Chicago. In the pale morning light of a November day, the city seemed to be made up of shades of brown, beige and gray. Though there wasn't any snow on the ground, the scent of winter was in the air, cool, and crisp. A snowstorm couldn't be far away.

By then I'll be safely back in New York, and this whole thing will be over. Genie tucked the fur throw more securely around her, as if it could shield her from the world.

She closed her eyes, mentally reviewing the countless bits of information in her head. *Be cool. Think before you speak. Don't do anything to make anyone suspect.*

She felt the limousine slow, then stop. Opening her eyes, she prepared to face the day.

"Madam?" The chauffeur held open the door.

"Thank you." She looked up at him from underneath her lashes as her sister had taught her, amazed to see the older man flush a deep shade of red, then grin idiotically.

Maybe Valerie had something here.

She was met in front of the brick building by a young man who took her to the correct studio through a maze of uninteresting hallways, past countless doors. Genie didn't pay attention to where she was going—they'd have to give her a guide at the end of the day.

"Your dressing room." The young man motioned toward a door.

"Thank you." She bestowed a dazzling smile on him and watched as he flushed and scampered away.

Well, well, well. This might turn out to be quite a lot of fun.

She quickly seated herself at the lighted mirror, took off her fur cape and combed out her hair. Checking her makeup, and satisfied with her appearance, she glanced up at the clock on the wall.

Eight in the morning. An ungodly hour by any standard, but anyone in the entertainment business knew it was par for the course.

Not wanting to wrinkle the back of her dress, she stood up and leaned against the counter.

A few minutes later she heard a timid knock on the door.

"Come in."

A petite woman with ash-blond hair and friendly blue eyes opened the door, balancing a tray in her hands. "Hi." Her voice was breathy, nervous. "You must be Valerie Bouchet." The end of her sentence came out a high-pitched squeak.

Genie smiled warmly. One thing her sister had drilled into her head was to be polite to everyone. "Yes. And you're—"

"Anne Tolman. Pierce Stanton's personal secretary." She set the tray down and held out her hand. Genie took it and squeezed it gently.

"You've saved my life. I hate getting up this early, and coffee can only help."

Anne expertly poured a single cup of coffee. As she set it down on the counter by the mirror, she eyed Genie curiously.

Understanding at a glance, Genie explained. "It's the material of this dress. It wrinkles so easily I can't sit down."

"Why don't you take it off? You don't go on for another hour."

Genie sighed, thinking wistfully of her faded jeans and oldest sweatshirt. "I think I will."

Once divested of her dress, she sat down in a chair in front of the mirror and began to enjoy her breakfast. The black silk slip, deeply trimmed with lace, shimmered like a liquid flame as she moved her arm, reaching for a hot cinnamon roll.

Anne stood by silently. Genie wondered what was wrong with the woman until comprehension dawned.

"Won't you join me, Anne? I'd be delighted if you would."

The blond woman blushed prettily, then took a seat and poured herself a cup of coffee. Taking another cinnamon roll and placing it on a napkin, she sat back in her chair as if she were relaxing for the first time that day.

They ate in silence for a few seconds, then Anne spoke.

"Valerie, I hope you won't mind my saying this, but my mother and I read all your books, and we just love the way you write." Anne paused for a second to catch her breath, then flushed even pinker. "I've brought a copy of my favorite, *Fast Lane.* If you wouldn't mind signing it..."

Genie felt her stomach twist as she set her coffee cup down carefully. Suddenly she felt very strange about her part in Valerie's deception. It was one thing as an intellectual concept, another when it involved people as nice as Anne.

"Of course I will," she replied, trying to inject vitality into her voice.

Anne dug into her purse and extracted two copies of Valerie's latest paperback. "My mother's name is Ellen, if you could just—"

"Of course." *Oh, Al, if you could see me now, signing my first autograph. You're right, fame is nothing like I'd ever expected it to be....*

Her thoughts were interrupted as the dressing-room door opened and a man with ice-blue eyes glanced around it. "Anne, where did you put—" He stopped talking as his eyes came to rest on Genie, clad only in her black silk slip, nylons and high heels.

He took a leisurely, insulting perusal of her body, and when their eyes met, there was a look Genie couldn't fathom in the depths of his eyes. She felt her stomach contract, her heartbeat speed up. The expression in his eyes seemed part desire, part contempt. Or was she imagining things again?

Without a word he shut the door, much more firmly than necessary, with a quick strong movement that suggested energy repressed.

It had happened so quickly, in the space of less than a minute.

"Oh, my God," Anne said quietly. "That was Pierce."

Though her body felt strangely weak and light, Genie waved her hand, consciously mimicking a gesture of Valerie's. "Not to worry." She gave Anne a devilish grin. "At least I was wearing clean underwear."

Anne stared at her in amazement, then started to laugh. Genie knew she'd made a friend.

Half an hour later, Genie put her dress back on, then Anne took her to the makeup man. He covered the neck of Genie's gown carefully, then went to work with his special brand of wizardry.

Afterward, a tall, dark-haired woman with a clipboard led her to a room, then gave her the glass of cold water she requested. Aside from a couch and a few nondescript chairs, the room also contained a television monitor and a mirror. Genie knew this was where she would wait until Pierce Stanton himself appeared on the screen. *Why didn't he welcome me to the show this morning?* she thought suddenly.

She studied him on the screen. He was an impressive male animal. Raven-black hair, and those eyes! She watched the way his tall, graceful body moved in the expensive gray suit. When he moved, he did so with a powerful energy, as if too much of the time he held back and had to relieve himself in motion if possible. Very exciting.

"Ladies and gentlemen, we have a very special guest here this week. She's one of the best-selling novelists in the world. I'd like you to welcome Valerie Bouchet."

Genie squared her shoulders, drew herself up to her full height of five three, and as someone parted the curtains, she swept regally out onto the stage, her scarlet silk gown shimmering underneath the hot studio lights.

There was a collective gasp from the audience as she walked gracefully up to Pierce Stanton, took both hands he offered her, raised her cheek for his brief kiss, then pirouetted and sat down on the seat next to his desk. The long skirt of her gown billowed out over the chair and part of the carpeted platform, and she spent the next few seconds tucking and arranging it before she looked up into his eyes.

What she saw shocked her. Contempt, plain and simple. But just as quickly, he masked it with a bland smile and directed his comments to the audience.

"What a dress, huh?"

Audience laughter rippled throughout the studio. Genie breathed deeply, trying to still her racing heartbeat. This was more than just simple stage fright. Her instincts were screaming at her. Something was wrong. Terribly wrong.

She studied her host. Pierce Stanton was taller than he appeared to be on television, five ten at least. His black hair was thick and straight, cut short, in a classic style that emphasized his bone structure. He had a strong, tense jaw, a straight nose and high cheekbones. It was an arrogant, classical face. A rich face. This man had grown up with money.

But his eyes, icy blue, were his best feature. They made his face come alive, hinted at intense passion below the surface. They held a suppressed energy, like the sky before a storm. Sharp, intelligent eyes that saw quickly to the heart of any matter.

Relentless eyes.

"Did you have a good flight in from Kennedy?" He seemed the perfect host, as if they were attending a private party and he was determined to see she had a good time.

Genie lowered her voice, pitched it so it came out smooth and husky. "Yes, I did."

"Nothing quite as stormy as in one of your novels." He smiled, but the smile didn't reach those eyes.

"No." She waited, realizing she was holding her breath.

"I'm happy to have you here with us today, Valerie."

I'll just bet you are.

"As you and your many fans know, each of your novels has made the New York Times best-seller list. Your books have sold in the millions, and whoever publishes your next novel can be guaranteed a best-seller." He smiled again. Those teeth. Genie was reminded of a wolf she'd once seen in a children's theatrical production of *Peter and the Wolf.*

His next question caught her completely off guard. "So how does it feel to be, as some of your most virulent critics have tagged you, a literary prostitute?"

She stared at him, stunned. Pierce Stanton was known for causing controversy on his show, but with his last question he'd gone a bit too far.

Though she wanted to take the glass of ice water on his desk and pour it over his finely-boned face until he was as frozen as his eyes, she restrained herself.

You cannot make a scene.

"Define prostitute." Her voice was a husky whisper.

The audience loved her reaction. She could hear a few laughs, a whistle or two. Valerie Bouchet was turning out to be just as feisty as any of her heroines.

Pierce seemed taken aback for just an instant. But he rallied quickly. "Someone who sells herself for money."

"I'd modify that definition a little." Though Genie was nervous, her intuition told her Pierce was attracted to her. She decided to test the waters. Leaning forward, she gave him a generous view of her cleavage as she flicked her mane of hair over her bare shoulders. "I'd define a prostitute as someone who takes money for something she or he essentially doesn't like to do." She looked up at him from underneath her lashes. "And I like what I do." She paused for effect. "Very much."

The audience applauded, and Pierce smiled. "Touché, Valerie."

Genie leaned back in her chair, but she didn't give herself the luxury of relaxing. This man was out to get her. But why?

"Your heroines are very strong, assertive women. Would you say you write for the modern liberated woman of today?"

There didn't seem to be any trick to this question. "Yes."

"So it follows you don't have much empathy for the woman who has children and makes homemaking her career."

Did Val say that? "I'm sorry you assume so. I can assure you I have nothing but admiration for any woman who chooses to remain at home."

"Yet you write about women who go after their men, sometimes at the expense of ruining the families involved."

Which book was that? For an instant, Genie panicked. Then her preparation took over. "You're referring to my novel *Child of Desire.* My heroine, Serita, falls in love with a married man, but she doesn't let herself love him until it's very clear there's nothing between Joshua and his wife.'' She sat back in her chair and eyed him steadily. ''Is there anything else you'd like to ask me about married women in my novels?''

He changed tactics smoothly. ''A large part of your popularity seems to stem from your extremely erotic love scenes.''

She nodded, wondering what he was getting at now. All her instincts were attuned to him. They were fighters in a private ring, on public display.

''Don't you think this leads to a glorification of sex, to an expectation that can lead someone astray?''

Where her sudden burst of audacity came for, Genie never knew. Quite deliberately, she leaned forward and touched his arm, stroked it through the fine wool of his jacket. ''One thing I've *never* been accused of is exaggerating.'' She smiled slowly, letting each bit of her expression dazzle him. ''And I think the higher your...expectations, the more effort you put into something. Don't you agree?''

The audience clapped, and Genie turned her attention to them, giving them a smile. She had them. *I could learn to love this,* Genie mused. It was a heady feeling, power. Valerie and the audience against Pierce Stanton, round one.

He turned toward the camera with an easy smile. ''Whatever my expectations, I think we'd better break for a commercial.''

As soon as they were no longer on camera, a makeup man hurried onto the set and dusted both their faces with powder. Genie took a quick sip of water before he reapplied her lipstick. Pierce remained silent, but she could feel him watching her.

What was the matter with him? Genie felt the craziest mixture of feelings. She knew he resented her, but she had seen attraction in his eyes. Grudging attraction. But how could he have decided so much about her—he'd only met her today! Did Pierce Stanton always make such snap judgments about his guests?

Genie knew she wasn't going to ask him. Her job was to give one week's worth of good interviews. Nothing more or less. But she'd be damned if she'd let this man ride roughshod all over her, even in the name of television sensationalism.

Relentless as ever, he was ready with another round of questions when the cameras started rolling again.

"Of all the books you read when you were a child, which influenced you most?"

This seemed safe enough. Almost bland. Genie searched quickly for what Valerie had told her. "Margaret Mitchell's *Gone with the Wind.*" She sat forward slightly, wanting to give him another chance.

"I see." Pierce's tone was that of an English headmaster, and Genie felt she was the recalcitrant student who was about to be punished. He sat back, deliberately putting space between them. "And yet Scarlett O'Hara has got to be one of the first-class bitches of all time."

Genie felt her cheeks begin to flush angrily under her makeup. If there was one thing she refused to tolerate, it was deliberately belittling someone else's work. She saw it all the time in her own world—theatrical actors who made fun of television actors, who made fun of commercial actors. She couldn't stand that attitude in anyone. Pierce Stanton and his condescending questions were beginning to rankle her.

She fluttered her lashes slightly. "I'm afraid I don't

follow you, Mr. Stanton. Would you be so kind as to repeat the question?''

His blue eyes seemed frozen. ''What I'm trying to say is—you have a tremendous opportunity to influence your audience, yet the role model you look for in a heroine is a woman who is in love with another woman's husband.''

There's something going on here I don't understand. ''What makes Scarlett such an incredible character is that she's human.'' *Which you, Mr. Stanton, most certainly are not.* ''I was swept up with Scarlett because she's a realistically drawn character, with complex feelings and emotions.''

''So you're saying you enjoy writing about women like Scarlett?''

''Yes. I like characters that are well drawn.'' Genie paused, then said lightly, ''I get the feeling you think I should be wearing a scarlet letter on my bosom.'' She cast her eyes downward, demurely, noticing that his eyes were caught and held by her breasts, pushed slightly upward by her bra.

''A scarlet dress will do,'' he said testily. Pierce looked away from her, toward the camera. ''And now we have to break for another commercial.''

Quietly seething inside, Genie was too proud to let him see how his remark had upset her. Besides, she'd seen Valerie laugh off much worse statements. She kept her face a cool, impenetrable mask as she took another sip of water to relieve her tight throat.

Let him know he's nothing special—he's not getting to you. ''I've enjoyed our little conversation so far, Mr.—''

The chilling glance he gave her stopped Genie in midsentence. She felt he had stripped her to the bone and found her disgusting. His open contempt amazed her.

She stopped talking abruptly, glanced away.

The last half of the program was devoted to taking calls from readers and answering audience questions. Genie was astounded to find out how well loved her sister was, how her novels had changed lives. After one woman in the studio finished her story about how *Paradise,* one of Valerie's latest novels, had saved her marriage, Genie found herself near tears.

But when taping was finished, Genie walked off the set without a backward glance. Stopping at her dressing room just long enough to retrieve her fur and bag, she headed through the maze of halls, her head held high, her heels clicking furiously. Pierce Stanton was absolutely crazy if he thought his private little war would make for an interesting program! How could he deliberately set out to make her feel so uncomfortable—so *insulted!* She'd seen him on television before, and he exuded charm, sophistication and a relaxed masculinity. Why wasn't he the same way with her—with Valerie?

The drive back to her hotel suite seemed longer than this morning. Perhaps it was the headache pounding behind her temples or the anger boiling in her blood. Who did Pierce Stanton think he was, treating her that way in front of the millions who watched his show? Though she'd answered his questions with spirit and intelligence, Genie knew she could have given a better interview if she hadn't been feeling as if she were tiptoeing through a mine field.

PIERCE SAT BACK in his office chair, his hands linked behind his neck, eyes closed. Why did Valerie have to be so damned attractive? There had been nothing in her photo to prepare him for the reality of the woman. She exuded warmth, charm and honesty. He couldn't picture her with Barbara's husband, Robert, as the latest in her entourage. Why had she put up with him?

She seemed so young. There was a freshness and innocence about her that no amount of surgery or cosmetics could account for.

And he'd been attracted to her from the first moment he'd seen her in the dressing room.

It was because she was undressed. You'd have to have been a damned corpse not to feel anything! He could remember her so easily, her softly curved body almost totally exposed underneath the thin silken slip. The deep lace border had done nothing to hide the fullness of her breasts, the clean white line of her throat. And those legs—

Pierce was disgusted with the familiar tightening of his body. Desire. He felt unclean, as if he were like his brother-in-law, rutting after anything in a skirt.

He'd shamed her. He'd seen the surprise on her face, the astonishment as he'd thrown first one question at her, then the next. Right about now, she'd have to be back in her hotel suite wondering what the devil he was up to!

And the damnedest thing was, he was the last person who could have told her.

AS GENIE RELAXED in the large marble tub, her black hair pinned up on top of her head with carved ivory pins, she played back the entire day in her mind.

He had gone after her, there was no doubt about it. Pierce had quite cruelly asked her deliberately provocative questions. His rudeness was intolerable. He seemed inhuman, his face tight and drawn, as if he had held himself in check. But if he'd been restraining himself today, she hoped she'd never have to face him when he decided to really go after her!

Everything he'd done had deliberately kept a distance between them. She wasn't looking forward to tomorrow, or the rest of the week. How could she possibly be comfortable while constantly wondering what he was going to fire at her next?

The man didn't make sense. The Pierce Stanton she'd watched on television had a talent for drawing people out, giving them permission to voice their deepest thoughts. It was what made his style of interviewing so satisfying to watch. But today—Genie felt her interview had resembled a cruel satirization on a late-night comedy show.

She sank lower in the fragrant water, willing her tense body to relax, deciding to forget about Pierce for the moment. She glanced around the opulent bathroom, mentally comparing the luxury of her surroundings with her small studio in New York. Half the time she was lucky if she *had* hot water. Or enough water pressure.

She had to talk to Valerie. Her sister had somehow known what was facing her in Chicago. She had known of Pierce's intense dislike. And she'd let her walk right into it.

Genie sighed as she stepped out of the tub. She should have listened to her instincts. But as usual, she'd acted impulsively. There was nothing for her to do but call Valerie and demand an end to this farce.

After wrapping herself in a thick terry towel, she

dialed her sister's number. Mimi, Valerie's maid, answered.

"Hi, Mimi. She's not in? Do you know when she'll be back?" Genie sank back into the soft mattress with a sigh. Where was Valerie? If she knew Val, she'd want to go over her performance on the talk show. And why hadn't her sister prepared her for her obnoxious host? There were several questions Genie wanted answers to.

Afterward she called Al. And charged it on Valerie's phone credit card.

"Hey, Genie." He sounded relieved. "You really held your own out there. Chaplin and I watched it this afternoon."

She could feel tears stinging her eyes. More than anything, Genie wanted to hop on the first flight back to New York. Escape and forget the rest of the week.

"Is he usually so rude?" Though she'd caught several of his shows before flying out of New York, she had never seen Pierce as antagonistic as he seemed today.

"Genie, I watch him all the time, but I've never seen him this way. Look," Al said soothingly, "he probably had a bad day. And after all, you're not out there as Genie, you're out there as Valerie. So he's trying to make an ass out of Valerie, not you."

Genie digested this bit of information in silence, then blurted out, "So how come I get the feeling Val's making an ass out of me?"

Chapter Three

After the second taping, Genie virtually dragged herself in the door. Taking a quick shower, she crawled into bed and pulled the covers over her head, totally exhausted.

Pierce Stanton, I'm going to kill you.

His questions had bordered on the ridiculous. He seemed obsessed with humiliating her, emphasizing the fact that her novels were ruining the moral fiber of the country.

He's going to have to lighten up, and fast.

She was asleep when the phone rang. Genie reached for it blindly and knocked it to the floor.

"'lo?" Her voice was husky with sleep.

"Valerie?" The voice on the other end of the line was deep and masculine.

"Who?" Then Genie remembered who it was she was supposed to be. She sat up in bed, swinging her legs over the side. "Yes, this is she."

"I'm downstairs in the lobby. I'd like to take you to dinner tonight." Pierce. She could almost see the steel in his intense eyes.

Genie covered the mouthpiece of the phone and sat very still. It was bad enough she had to put up with him on the set. But to accept his invitation bordered on the masochistic!

"What makes you think I'd want to be in the same room with you?" she countered. "I'm just curious." As she spoke, she glanced at the bedside clock. She'd slept the entire day away!

"Look." The words seemed forced out of him. "I'm sorry about what I did to you today. We...have to talk."

Genie thought about this for a moment. It couldn't hurt. Not when she had to face him for the rest of the week, starting tomorrow morning.

She glanced up at the large mirror over the dresser, studied herself with horror. Without any makeup on, she looked about twenty years old. She needed time to complete her disguise.

"Give me fifteen minutes and I'll meet you in the lobby."

"Fine."

She hung up the phone, then raced into the bathroom and washed her face. Applying her makeup skillfully, she sculpted her face, playing with lights and shadows until she resembled Valerie Bouchet. Changing into a pair of navy wool pants and an oversized navy-and-winter-white sweater, she grabbed a mink jacket, her key and wallet, then headed for the door.

Pierce rose from his chair as soon as she entered the lobby, and Genie had to admit he did look handsome in dark-gray pants and a gray tweed pullover. Dressed casually, he didn't look as ferocious. He ran his hand quickly over the hair above his right temple, as if the gesture relaxed him. She thought she detected a slightly vulnerable look in his eyes for an instant. A softening of his features. But vulnerability from Attila the Hun? Before Genie was sure, his expression changed, and back in place was the self-assured, controlled mask he used on the show.

"Thank you for meeting me," he said quietly when she fell into step beside him.

"My appetites usually overrule my common sense," Genie replied, careful to use her sister's husky voice. For some perverse reason, she couldn't resist baiting him. She wanted to break through his mask, wanted to see that vulnerable expression again.

He seemed to consciously stifle a retort, then took a deep breath as the two of them walked through the revolving door and out of the overheated lobby into the brisk evening air.

"Have you ever had Chicago-style pizza?" Pierce's voice sounded slightly formal, though his question was casual.

Pizza? From this man? It was the last thing she would have thought someone as formal as Pierce would enjoy. For some reason she'd expected an expensive restaurant on top of one of Chicago's many skyscrapers. Soft lighting, an elegant atmosphere and the twinkling city spread out at their feet.

But pizza?

He smiled, and Genie was amazed at how much more relaxed he looked. "How does it sound to you?"

"Fine." She was starving. The last thing Genie could remember eating was the coffee and roll Anne had brought into her dressing room this morning.

Nancy's Pizzeria was located in the back of a shopping center, fifteen miles out of the city. It was the kind of place Genie loved, unpretentious and simple. She could picture herself and Al here much more readily than Pierce and anyone. The fragrance of basil and oregano filled the air as Pierce opened the door for her.

"Hey, Pierce, how are you tonight?" a heavy-set man called out. He was behind a wooden counter at the front of the restaurant, ladling thick tomato sauce over a circle of dough. He grinned when he saw them.

Pierce smiled again, and Genie watched his face carefully. She *hadn't* been imagining it! Why didn't this man smile more often? It changed his face, softened the intensity of his eyes, eased the lines around his mouth. It made him look human.

"Just fine, Stefano. How are you?"

"Okay. The usual?" Stefano's dark eyes twinkled mischievously. "That's one beautiful lady you have with you."

"Yes, she is," Pierce replied quietly.

Genie was subdued as she and Pierce seated themselves at a booth. He seemed different, not at all like the arrogant talk-show host earlier in the day. Maybe it was the sweater.

She let him order, wanting to maintain this rare moment of tranquillity between them. While he spoke to their waitress, she studied him. He was good-looking, with a classic bone structure that screamed good breeding. Dark Irish: the contrast of raven-black hair, ivory skin and icy-blue eyes made his looks striking, not subtle. His mouth was firm and sensual, and Genie found herself wondering what his kiss would be like.

At that exact moment their waitress turned away toward the kitchen and Pierce looked right at her.

Genie had the most disconcerting feeling that he knew what she'd been thinking. Or was he thinking the same thing? Determined not to feel embarrassed, she tilted her chin up. Why did she have to feel so defensive? He couldn't possibly know what she'd been thinking.

She wanted him to look away first, and he did. His eyes dropped to her mouth, studying it for several seconds. Genie caught her breath, then bit down on her lower lip. He raised his eyes back to hers.

"Are you hungry?" The simple question was suffused with erotic content by the look in his blue eyes. All iciness gone, they were alive and relaxed. He seemed determined to enjoy himself with her. Genie decided to play along.

"Very." She glanced away from him, down to his hands. He had large hands, with long, sensitive-looking fingers. She wondered what they would feel like on the small of her back, pressing her closer to his body as he enfolded her in his arms....

You've been reading too many of Val's novels.

Stefano brought a bottle of wine to their booth, and Genie watched the men as they bantered back and forth with each other. There was genuine liking and respect in Pierce's eyes as he gazed up at the older man. Stefano seemed like a father to him. Genie was surprised to hear Pierce speak quietly in Italian, the sounds fluent and melodic. She sensed he wasn't trying to impress her—he and Stefano were obviously old friends.

She tasted the wine, then nodded her head in answer to the question in Pierce's eyes.

"It's very good."

He filled her glass the rest of the way, then set the bottle down and leaned back in his seat, his stance deceptively relaxed. When his long legs bumped hers underneath the table, Genie jerked her knees away.

"You were feisty this morning," he observed.

"You must bring out the best in me." Genie certainly wasn't going to make this easy for him. Was he going to apologize?

"I like a woman with spirit," he said softly as he raised his wineglass to her.

"I'm married, Mr. Stanton." Genie took refuge in her role. Certainly Valerie wouldn't be caught dead seriously flirting with him. She raised her hands slowly, and the plain gold band Val insisted she wear caught the dim light and gleamed.

"I know." The look in his eyes was unfathomable.

Their salads arrived. Genie had chosen creamy garlic dressing, and it was pungent, with plenty of bite. *That* ought to discourage any fooling around!

She could barely eat, she was so conscious of the man sitting across from her. Though he didn't really *do* anything that could be construed as overtly sexual, a charge was in the air, enveloping her and making her feel that she was being pulled toward him against her will.

Finishing half her salad, Genie pushed the plate away and folded her hands in front of her. She resisted the urge to pick up her other fork and doodle nervously on the red-and-white-checked tablecloth.

"Look, Mr. Stanton..."

"Call me Pierce. Please."

"Look, Pierce. For whatever reason, it's pretty clear you don't like me."

He narrowed his eyes. "Very smart."

She unclasped her hands and reached for her wine. "Since we have to do three more shows before I fly back to New York, would it be presumptuous of me to ask why you've chosen me as your latest crusade?" Before he had a chance to reply, she raced on. "I've seen your show, and I know you like to play devil's advocate, but I found this morning...difficult."

"So did I."

His quiet open admission was not what she had expected. As she was about to reply, a waitress arrived with their pizza. She sliced it and dished it up onto earthenware plates, then set the rest of the pizza on a small stand. When she left, Pierce resumed their conversation.

His voice was soft, but she heard every word. "By the time we're finished tonight, you're going to know everything you have to know." His face was that smooth, blank mask Genie was growing to hate.

I feel like I'm in the middle of one of Val's novels, she thought wildly. *Nothing is worth it, not even pizza this good.* But at the thought of her sister, Genie remembered whom she was supposed to be portraying. It did no good to let *her* feelings get in the way. Valerie's novels were populated with feisty, fiery heroines. And she was an actress, wasn't she? Valerie wouldn't shy from Pierce Stanton no matter what the circumstances.

Neither would she.

She reached for her slice of pizza. It was cool enough to handle with her fingers. *To hell with formalities, I'm hungry.* She picked it up and began to eat.

"You act as if you're starved," he commented.

She swallowed. "I am. The last thing I ate today was a roll in my dressing room."

She regretted her reference the minute the words were out of her mouth.

"Ah, yes, the dressing room. How could I forget?" She could tell from the look in his eyes he was remembering the first time he had seen her, in her black silk slip.

For someone with his iron control of facial expression, he sure does have expressive eyes.

Genie wished she could say something to ease the tension. What could he think of her? She hadn't reacted the way he probably thought proper. No doubt he thought she should have made a fuss and reached for her dress. How could she tell him that as an actress she was used to changing clothes in any conceivable situation? It wasn't that she was casual about her body; but she certainly wasn't ashamed of it.

They ate the rest of their meal in silence, and Genie wondered all the while what "everything you have to know" could possibly mean. What had Valerie gotten her into this time, and why hadn't her sister coached her on this part of her assignment?

When the bill arrived, they both reached for the plastic tray.

"Listen, Pierce," Genie said, covering his hand with hers. "I'm sure I make a great deal more than you do. Let me cover this in return for your gracious hospitality." She couldn't resist the subtle dig. Something deep inside made her want to get back at him for all the cracks he'd made at her on his show. With her new, more sensuous image and Valerie's American Express gold card in her wallet, she felt a supreme confidence.

His eyes narrowed as he watched her. "I asked you out. The least I can do is pay for it."

She knew to argue with this man would be pointless. "As you wish."

She followed him outside to the parking lot, fastening her fur jacket against the cold, pushing her hands into the silk-lined pockets. Was it possible this city was colder than New York? Maybe it had something to do with the emotional climate.

When they entered the lobby of her hotel, Genie turned to Pierce and extended her hand. "Thanks for seeing me home. I'll see you at the studio tomorrow."

"I'll walk you to your room."

At her doorway, Genie inserted her key and opened the door, then turned slightly, blocking the open entrance with her body, ready to give him a final farewell.

He was looking at her as if he couldn't quite put the pieces of a puzzle together.

"Well...good night." She held out her hand.

"We have to talk."

"I don't think we have anything more to say to each other." Genie's voice was calm, revealing none of the tension she felt inside. It wasn't that she was scared of having Pierce in her room. He seemed an extremely proper man, and she couldn't see him hauling her off into the bedroom. But she didn't want to hear what he had to say. She had a feeling she wasn't going to be overjoyed.

"Yes, we do." Without further discussion, he guided her into the suite, the palm of his hand firm against her back.

She deliberately sat at the far end of the couch overlooking Lake Michigan's shoreline. Pierce's blue eyes were distant as he sat down across from her. She hoped whatever he had to say could be said quickly.

"Let's make this fast. I have a limousine coming in less than five hours."

"You're nothing at all like I expected you to be," he said quietly.

She stiffened slightly. Was he beginning to suspect? She'd have to watch herself. Speaking calmly, she replied, "What do you mean?"

"From what Barbara—" He stopped, looking as if he hadn't wanted to say what he'd said. Leaning back in his chair, he laced his fingers behind his head and watched her like a cat with a particularly fascinating bird.

Genie almost squirmed with impatience.

"Does the name Robert Tyler mean anything to you?" He was watching her face carefully.

Damn! Genie couldn't shake the feeling that the masquerade was over. What had tipped Pierce off? She kept her voice carefully modulated when she answered him. "Should it?"

His eyes seemed to grow darker, and Genie knew he was angry with her.

"What is it with you, don't you even remember their names?"

"What are you talking about?" She tried to remain calm, but she could detect a slight quaver in her voice. What had Valerie gotten her into?

"Robert Tyler. Vice-president of the Lakeshore Bank. You met him at a party your publisher threw at the American Booksellers Association convention. He asked you to stay over a few extra days, and you complied."

Complied. What a horrible, sleazy word. Did this man know Valerie's entire life story? He certainly knew more than she did! She'd have to stall for time.

"Ah, the ABA." Her mind seemed to be working in slow motion.

"So you remember him?" Pierce's voice had a distinct edge to it.

She had to play along. "Yes, I think I do."

A look of utter disgust crossed his expressive features. "Did he tell you he was married?"

She couldn't disguise her shock.

"So you didn't know. That makes it all even more interesting."

Genie's head was beginning to throb painfully. More than anything, she wanted to retreat to her bedroom. "I'd like you to leave now." She stood up and walked to the door, pulling it open and making a sweeping gesture with her hand.

He studied her for a long moment, then rose slowly from his chair. As he walked toward her, Genie held tightly to the doorknob. He seemed overpowering in the silent room.

But he didn't leave. Instead, he took her hand and pried it from the knob. Closing the door, he backed her up against it.

"If I go now, will I get my answers in the morning?"

"Yes." She was relieved he was leaving. Something had been building between them all day, and Genie wanted to diffuse the tension before it exploded, engulfing them.

His eyes moved over her face; then his gaze settled on her mouth once again. Genie held herself perfectly still, wishing she hadn't made up her lips with the shimmering gloss. She knew they looked soft, sensual, provocative.

And Pierce was obviously no saint. He lifted his gaze to her eyes and for a moment seemed torn, as if conflicting emotions were raging through him. He took her hand and held it tightly in his.

"One more question." His voice was firm.

"Then will you leave?" Genie knew her reply sounded breathless, but she was having trouble forcing air into her lungs when Pierce looked at her.

"May I kiss you?" His question sounded loud in the quiet room.

Genie stared at him, shocked. A part of her wanted to run into his arms and test the attraction between them, see if he could make her feel as wild as he did simply by looking at her. Another part of her knew it was madness. But she couldn't stop staring at him. There was a strange, quiet moment in which they looked at each other, and it was as if a silent bond had formed between them. Genie suddenly realized she didn't want to run away from the message in his eyes. Everything logical warned her to walk away from him, but she couldn't. The fascination she had for this man was simply too strong. Her eyes moved down to his well-shaped lips, and she sighed. The unconscious gesture parted her lips, and she wet them with the tip of her tongue. Very slowly, she nodded her head.

Something had leaped up between them, as quickly lit as tinder in a fire. A quick flash, the barest of kindling. Yet Genie was certain Pierce had felt it, too. She sensed it in the way he moved slowly toward her. He looked as if he was as caught up in the feeling as she was.

He slid his fingers past her cheeks, up into her hair, until he cradled her jaw in the palms of his hands. The warmth of his touch seemed to sing through her blood, and she took another breath, anxious.

Pierce lowered his head very slowly, then touched his lips to hers.

Genie felt as if someone had ripped away all her defenses, leaving raw emotion exposed. The minute he touched her, her body began to respond, going all soft and liquid, yearning toward him. She managed to steel herself before she leaned against him, to hold herself rigidly erect. If she touched that hard body, she knew she wouldn't want to stop with a kiss.

He teased her lips apart, and they responded willingly, letting him ease his tongue inside and explore. She'd stopped fighting herself, pushed away all thoughts of a moment of reckoning. She wanted to be held in his arms, was excited by the very fact he'd asked her for a kiss. He had to feel it, too; it wasn't possible that so powerful an emotion could be felt by only one person. It had to move him as well, flashing through his body like lightning arcing across a midnight sky.

Desire flowed through her body, quick and hot, causing her legs to start trembling and her breasts to ache. Though he was only touching her face, she wanted to press herself against him and give up all pretense of rational thought.

She felt his mouth tremble slightly against hers; then he became more the aggressor, tightening his hold, making her bend her head back and take the full force of his passion. Genie responded to this man, to the wild sexuality he unleashed inside her. She touched his tongue with the tip of her own and heard him groan, deep in his throat. A primitive, muffled sound. It made her feel strangely triumphant.

She didn't want Pierce to be controlled when he kissed her.

He broke the kiss abruptly, keeping his hands on her face. Genie closed her eyes and tried to will the sensuous warmth to stop blooming, stop suffusing her body with traitorous urges. The contrast in Pierce was exciting: reserved one minute, hot and passionate the next.

She opened her eyes to see him breathing deeply, his face flushed, a lock of his perfectly cut hair falling over his high forehead. Had she done that? Even now, looking at him, she had to clench her hands into fists, resist the urge to run her fingers through his hair, down over his shirtfront to the buttons and beneath....

He dropped his hands from her face, took both her hands in his. She looked away from him, suddenly ashamed of her response. There had been none of Valerie in that. Only Genie.

"Did you feel it?" he asked quietly, slowly pulling her unresisting body against his.

She nodded.

"I want to kiss you again."

She didn't seem to have the strength of will to refuse. He wrapped his arms around her, his cheek against her hair.

"You're going to let me." There was a rough tenderness in his voice, and he made his request a statement, not a question.

She simply raised her face to his.

"Kiss me." His mouth moved to hers.

Genie felt her legs begin to tremble as he kissed her again. She touched his shoulders tentatively at first, then curled her fingers into the soft yarn of his pullover. She let him inside her mouth, let him caress her with tongue and lips, let him press her back against the door with his hips. His hands moved up, framing her face, turning it gently so he could continue the kiss without interruption.

She would have slid down the doorframe without his support. A soft strangled sound escaped past her lips as he threaded one of his hands through her hair, then lowered his mouth to her neck, teasing the sensitive flesh.

It was unbearably exciting, being this close to Pierce. His warm hand slipped underneath her sweater, moved slowly, sensuously up her rib cage, stroked up underneath her bra. He found the clasp with ease, freeing her breasts. He caressed them both, lightly, gently pinching the swollen tips between his thumb and forefinger, returning his mouth to hers.

She didn't want to stop what was happening. Genie had always read her sister's books with a certain suspicion, never quite believing the way the heroine relinquished herself to her lover. She'd always thought those parts the most unbelievable. Thus it came as a major shock when, for the first time in her life, the same feelings swept through her.

Pierce pushed the sweater up past her breasts, then lowered his dark head and took one of her nipples into his warm mouth. Genie cried out softly as the liquid touch sent tremors throughout her body. Without conscious thought, her hands went to his dark head and she clasped him tighter against her, not wanting him to stop giving her such exquisite sensations, as elusive as quicksilver. He fed her sensation, caressing the tip of her breast until heavy warmth suffused her limbs and she could only feel his hands, his mouth. As she moved her palms restlessly over the thick, silky hair on his head, she groaned softly. As if in answer to her unspoken plea, he moved to her other breast, drawing the tip into his mouth, pulling on it strongly.

Genie thought her legs were giving away, then realized he was lifting her up, carrying her down the hall to the bedroom. He set her down gently on the king-sized bed, his eyes never leaving her face. She watched him, her throat dry, as his long fingers quickly pulled off his sweater, then the button-down shirt underneath.

His chest was as she had imagined it, smoothly muscled and covered with dark hair. Without his sweater on, he looked larger, more primitive. The control she'd credited him with was being stripped away to reveal the sexual man beneath. He watched her as intently as she watched him, and the knowledge gave Genie a feeling of uncertainty, then elation. He was as intrigued with her as she with him.

Before he removed his pants, he lay down on the bed, gently pinning her beneath him.

She couldn't resist the urge to touch him, wanting to know everything about him. Wanting to know if she affected him the way he did her. She smoothed her fingertips over the muscles in his chest, then moved lower, not quite daring to touch him in a more intimate place.

He made her decision for her. Grasping her hand in his, he guided it down to his belt, then lower.

"Touch me," he whispered.

She was hesitant, so he pressed her fingers against his body and she felt the hot, hard flesh. He was fully aroused.

She looked up at his face. His eyes were narrowed, then he closed them, the cords in his throat standing out in sharp relief. Her touches were light and tentative until he put his hand back over hers and showed her how to stroke him.

"Yes. Oh, God. Valerie." His voice was husky with desire.

Valerie. She took her hand away from his and tried

to roll away from him. He pinned her easily underneath him, his hips hard and insistent against hers. Taking both her hands in one of his, he raised them up above her head.

"Valerie?" There was a question in his voice.

How had she gotten herself into this mess to begin with? Why did she have to pretend she was someone she wasn't? More than anything, Genie wanted to know this man intimately. The sexual connection between them burned hotly, couldn't be ignored.

But she couldn't do it as Valerie.

"Valerie?" he asked her again, more softly this time.

Hating herself, she started to cry, closing her eyes and letting the tears roll down her cheeks. All her frustration went into her tears as she simply opened up and let them come. She hated herself, she hated the situation and she almost hated Pierce for being so sensitive. Why wasn't he like one of the heroes in Valerie's books? Why didn't he take the decision out of her hands?

But he didn't. Pierce got up, slowly, looking as shaken as she felt. He turned his back to her, and she saw his muscles flex as he raised a shaking hand and ran it through his disheveled hair.

"I'm sorry, Valerie." It was all he said before he picked up his shirt and sweater and walked out of the room. Then she heard the sound of the door closing behind him.

When she stopped crying and trembling, Genie glanced at the bedside clock. Almost three in the morning! Well, Valerie would have to understand. Reaching for the phone, she dialed her sister's number.

Chapter Four

As Pierce drove swiftly back to his house in Evanston, he wondered what could have possessed him to behave the way he had with Valerie. He'd despised Robert for fooling around while married—how here he was, trying to make love with a married woman!

Nothing had seemed the same since he first met her. She'd assaulted his senses, broken through to his deepest feelings. Valerie Bouchet was the most desirable woman he'd ever met.

But it was more than that. Pierce sensed instinctively she had what he lacked—a passion for living. He couldn't remember the last time he'd felt this alive, this passionate. All he had to do was look at her, and feeling came rushing through him.

He could remember the exact moment he'd first seen her. His first glimpse of her face had been in the dressing-room mirror, but his eyes had been captured by the smooth skin of her back, accentuated by the black satin slip. A man who was carefully controlled, he was shocked when all control vanished.

He wanted to drag her off to bed. He wanted to see some of that passion for living in his bedroom.

Within minutes he was turning into the driveway of

his house. The light above the solid oak door beamed brightly, warmly. Everything was exactly as he'd left it this morning on his way to work.

But nothing would ever be the same again.

THE NEXT MORNING Genie stared into the bathroom mirror and applied more concealer to disguise the dark circles developing under her eyes. She'd be putting it on with a trowel by the end of the week.

What could she have been thinking of? And why had Pierce acted that way? And Valerie—

She had demanded the truth from her sister and learned to her dismay that Valerie had had an affair with Robert Tyler, Pierce's brother-in-law. His sister, Barbara, had found out and divorced her husband.

Oh, what a tangled web we weave, she thought as she walked out into the living room and studied the next dress to be worn in the series of interviews. The décolletage was even more daring. It was a bugle-beaded gown, shot through with deep blue and silver. It molded her figure to perfection, but as Genie stared at the dress she wasn't at all sure she wanted to appear so vulnerable in front of Pierce.

Last night she'd been tempted to abandon the entire masquerade, but Valerie had won their argument. If she came back now, her sister assured her, Harold would wonder why and have to be told the truth.

"But why should it matter to him?" Genie argued. "This happened before you were married to Harold."

"But we were still involved! I had an argument with him before I left for the ABA, and I regret that slip with Robert. Genie, I never *told* Harold about it, and I don't want him to know. You know how jealous he is of me!"

She had continued to argue with her sister, but Valerie was clearly fighting for her life. When Genie tried to stand up to her sister, the fighting turned ugly.

"Okay, Genie. Come home, then. I expect my money back in full, plus what it cost me to outfit you. It should only take you the rest of your life."

Genie was staggered. "Val! You're not being fair! You didn't tell me the truth when I agreed to do this job or I never would have done it!"

Her sister sounded impatient. "Grow up, Genie. You want to be an actress, don't you? You have a choice—pay me back or walk out."

She closed her eyes tightly before she replied, and Pierce's face, shaken and pale from last night, flashed through her memory. "What you're telling me is that I have no choice, Val."

Her sister fairly purred her response. "I knew you'd come around to seeing things sensibly."

Genie thought back to their conversation as she stared at the dress. She was clad only in a complete body stocking and heels. The beaded dress would simply slide over her like a second skin. She sighed wearily as she contemplated the day ahead.

So here you are again, the strong one in the family. Making everything all right, except for you. Genie started as the phone rang.

"Hello?" Her voice was slightly raspy from her sleepless night.

"The limousine is waiting, Ms. Bouchet."

Angrily, she donned the dress, throwing the rest of her costume props into a large canvas bag. She'd make her transformation at the studio.

WHEN THE ALARM WENT OFF, Pierce was awake. He'd been up all night, trying to put together the puzzle that was Valerie.

She'd been vulnerable with him last night. If he'd needed one final clue proving she wasn't a hard, jaded woman, her response had given it to him. The way her mouth had opened beneath his, the look in her wide, dark eyes when he'd pressed her against the bed with his hips...

He swore softly as he swung out of bed and headed for the shower. A cold one, that was what he needed. As he turned on the water and stepped beneath the frigid, stinging spray, he thought about the questions he had set out on his desk before leaving his office yesterday.

They were still fairly abusive. He didn't feel he'd gotten beneath the façade to the woman she really was. Yet Pierce wasn't as sure of his game plan as he'd been before he'd kissed her. Who was Valerie Bouchet, really? She couldn't have faked a response like that.

She's married. That was the one indisputable fact that stood in the way of his taking her to bed and putting all his erotic dreams into action.

Angrily, he picked up the soap and began to lather his chest. *Keep that in mind the next time you feel like kissing her.*

''YOU LOOK WONDERFUL, Valerie,'' Anne said. ''Just like the woman on the cover of *Temptation's Promise.*''

Genie studied her appearance in the mirror. It was amazing what a chocolate croissant and a cup of good coffee could do for a person's disposition. Her black hair was pulled starkly off her face and braided with silver ribbons. The blue and silver of the beaded gown complemented her coloring perfectly. Silver heels and sapphire earrings completed the outfit.

If I can make it through the last three interviews, I can forget this whole thing ever happened, she lied to herself.

A soft knock at the door interrupted her thoughts, and the assistant producer walked in. "They're waiting for you. Oh, and—" Suddenly flustered, she pulled a copy of Valerie's newest novel from beneath her clipboard. "Would you autograph this today if you have time? If you would just put: 'To Chelley.'"

"Of course I will." *Be gracious, Genie. It's only your life that's falling apart.*

Pierce was nowhere to be seen backstage, and Genie was thankful. How could she face him without their roles on the talk show as a defense? She felt hot color rise up her neck as she remembered her response to his lovemaking. He'd been so responsive to her feelings, leaving before their mutual attraction had blazed out of control. She'd been beyond any control.

Accepting his invitation to dinner and letting him come upstairs to her suite had been the fatal error.

Never again.

"I'D LIKE YOU to once again welcome Valerie Bouchet."

Genie walked out from behind the curtain to enthusiastic applause. She settled herself carefully in the plush chair and awaited Pierce's first question with about as much enthusiasm as a child expecting a spanking.

He was perfectly in control, completely different from the passionate man she had been with last night.

How could his eyes appear so cool when she had seen them blaze with intense desire?

"Tell me, Valerie, do you feel women receive sexual satisfaction reading your books?"

She stared at him. He couldn't be serious. At that moment, her frustration peaked—Genie was impatient with the entire masquerade and decided to have some fun. Her dark-brown eyes twinkled devilishly. "That depends, Mr. Stanton. If you're hungry in the middle of the night, do you reach for a cookbook?"

The laughter was thunderous. She looked away before Pierce could catch her eye and smiled at the audience. *We're back where we started.*

But she'd let him know she wasn't going to tolerate any loaded questions. For the rest of the hour Pierce grilled her relentlessly, and she answered every question in detail.

As the program neared its end, he asked, "What's been the most rewarding aspect of your career?"

"The people. The people who wait twenty minutes in the rain when you come to do an autographing at their local bookstore. The women who write and let me know I entertained them for a few days, took them away from their troubles. And the other writers I know, who on the whole are very supportive. They're professional." She looked him squarely in the eye. *Why are we this way with each other? Why can't I just tell him who I am and be done with this whole thing?*

The third day of taping finished, Genie escaped to her dressing room once again. She was just getting ready to leave when she heard a tap on the door.

Pierce?

But it was Anne. "I was wondering... You're probably tired, but I thought since your hotel is part of the same building, maybe I could meet you at one of the restaurants in the Water Tower Place and we could have lunch together.''

The Ritz-Carlton Hotel was part of a massive grouping of stores, restaurants and offices that made up Water Tower Place on Michigan Avenue. Genie wouldn't even have to leave the structure to find a restaurant in the complex.

She thought quickly of all the little caring things Anne had done for her since she'd arrived at the studio on Monday. Besides, she liked her. And she had to do something to get her mind off Pierce. ''It sounds terrific. Just let me go back to my hotel and change.''

''There's a French café by the movie theater. I'll be there.''

Back in her suite, Genie carefully hung up her gown, took a quick shower, and changed into her serviceable black wool pants and a hand-knit angora sweater in black and red. Clipping silver hoops on her ears took a few more seconds; then she brushed out her braided hair and pulled it off her face with a clip.

Feeling more like Genie than she had since the first day she'd arrived in Chicago, she set off.

Anne proved to be a charming luncheon companion. And perceptive.

''You seem to be having a little trouble with Pierce,'' she remarked as they finished up their meal with café au lait and chocolate mousse.

''That's the understatement of the year.'' Genie tried not to think back to last night. That side of Pierce she liked. Too much. ''I think he took a violent dislike to me on sight.''

''I can't understand it,'' Anne said. She took another sip of her coffee. ''Usually he's so caring. He tries to make his guests look good.''

''I know.'' Genie took a quick bite of what was left of her mousse. ''I used to watch his show.'' *Never again.* But she wasn't sure if she would be angry or upset to see him on television once she was back in New York.

''I can't think of anything you're doing to rub him the wrong way.'' Anne wrinkled her brow, deep in thought.

No. I just slept with his brother-in-law, destroyed his sister's marriage—then had the gall to write a few best-sellers and make a ton of money. Why couldn't she have met Pierce Stanton under different circumstances? She could feel her cheeks start to heat up—if she'd met him under different circumstances she would have ended up in bed with him the first night they met! The attraction they had for each other was too intense.

''Does it bother you?'' Anne asked gently.

''Yes.'' Genie pushed her empty plate away from her. Whenever she was anxious, she ate. ''It bothers me a great deal.''

''You handle yourself beautifully, but it must be horrible having to deal with all the tension.''

''It is.'' Genie took a final sip of her coffee. ''If only I had some idea of the questions he was going to throw at me....'' Her voice trailed off as she studied Anne's ash-blond head. ''Maybe you can help me after all.''

''How?''

''How long have you worked for Pierce?''

''Since he started on the show—three years ago.''

''Then you must be familiar with his work habits.''

"Well...yes."

"How does he decide which questions to ask me?" *The million-dollar question.* If she could get this information out of Anne, maybe she could leave Chicago with shreds of her pride and self-confidence still intact. Genie could barely sit still as she saw comprehension dawn on Anne's pretty face.

"He...he works differently from most talk-show hosts. I know there isn't any panel of people who draw up the questions. Pierce writes them out on three-by-five cards, then shuffles them around and picks out the questions he thinks the audience will want answered. He tries to think like the viewer sitting at home. That's why he's been so successful."

"What happens next?"

"Then one of the secretaries types up the list he's chosen. That's what you see on his desk each day, on the set."

Genie decided to come straight to the point. "Could you get me a copy?"

"Well..."

"I promise to ship you and your mother first editions of the rest of my books. You'll get them as soon as I do."

Anne was beginning to waver.

"You'd get them months before they hit the stores." Genie could tell she was almost ready to capitulate. She pressed on. "Personally autographed. And I'll go wherever your mother lives and spend an afternoon with her." Genie felt desperate now. She needed this little edge to make it through the final days of taping.

Anne looked up, but her clear blue eyes were troubled. "I'll try. It's just that if Pierce ever finds out—"

"Let me handle Mr. Stanton," Genie said, with much more assurance than she felt.

PIERCE DIDN'T CALL HER that evening. And Genie tried not to admit to herself how much she wanted him to. After a quick nap to compensate for her sleepless night, she found herself pacing through her suite, pure restless energy and nerves. What was he thinking? Where was he? How did he have the power to invade her thoughts and leave her a mass of undirected emotion?

And why did she still want to see him so badly?

CALL HER.

Pierce stared at the phone in his den, then slowly lifted his hand until his fingers were curved around the receiver.

To apologize.

He grimaced, then let go of the receiver. Shifting in the leather chair next to the fireplace, he gazed into the waning fire.

The den was his refuge. It was the warmest room in the large mansion, and Pierce found comfort here. After his mother died, she had left the house to him. He had moved into it when he turned eighteen, his coming of age. He hadn't been able to leave his father's house fast enough.

Hard to believe we're in the same family.

His thoughts strayed to Valerie, to the night he had almost spent in her suite. *You could have had her. She wanted to make love as much as you did.*

But it wouldn't have been lovemaking, not on her side. The minute he had said her name, it was as if she remembered who she was. A married woman.

You're worse than Robert ever was, the thoughts you're thinking.

He sighed deeply, and Parrish, one of his golden retrievers, trotted over from in front of the fire and sat down by his chair, demanding to be petted. Pierce ran his fingers over the dog's silky fur, remembering the softness of Valerie's skin, the faint flush in her cheeks, the desire in her eyes....

Face reality. She has a husband. He sat up and walked over to the fireplace, closing the screen on the dying embers. If only he could put a damper on his own feelings so easily.

He'd never been as affected by a woman. And there had been quite a few in his life. He'd always managed to keep his distance, promised them nothing. Even with his brutal honesty, he'd always had women.

But none had ever filled the emptiness inside him.

Your thoughts are taking a decidedly morbid turn. He snapped his fingers, and Parrish and Jaime got up off the hardwood floor, following him into the kitchen. He let them out the back door for their last run of the evening and watched as they trotted out to the edge of the grounds, then disappeared into the thicket of oak trees.

After ten minutes, he whistled sharply and they came bounding back toward him, their tongues lolling out of their mouths, panting and woofing as they skidded into the kitchen.

The two dogs followed their master up the stairs as he headed toward his bedroom.

HE WAS RUNNING, running after the black-and-white ball, eagerly trying to take it from one of the other boys. The fall wind rushed to meet his face as he ran, and it felt good being outside again. He hadn't felt good in such a long time.

Then he had the ball and skillfully maneuvered it to the other end of the soccer court, where he gave it a final furious kick and scored a point.

Happy and exhausted, he headed for the sidelines, walking at a relaxed pace with his team.

"Pierce, look!" One of the boys from the opposing team had given him the clipping. He had smiled at him, but the boy merely looked uneasy and ran away in the opposite direction.

Then he read it. And stopped walking. And read it again. Trying to make sense of the blurred newsprint, the picture of his mother. But she was smiling in the picture, and he couldn't remember seeing her happy.

"Stanton, come on." His coach.

He turned and ran in the opposite direction, the clipping a wad of ink and paper in his clenched fist.

"Stanton!" The coach's voice grew fainter as he continued to run, his legs pistoning furiously, harder than he'd ever run in any game. Trying to outrace his feelings, exhaust himself so he wouldn't feel anything, wouldn't have to know....

He entered the woods at the edge of the academy still running full force. The trees closed over him, and he thought about climbing up the highest one and throwing himself down. Then he'd be with his mother again and they could never—

He tripped over a root and fell flat, smashing his face against the cold hard earth. He lay still as the pain washed over him. But he couldn't scream. His breath came in short, panting little sobs as he sat up, wiped the blood from his face.

Then he began to cry.

PIERCE SAT UP IN BED, gasping for breath. He reached out for the bedside lamp and turned it on. As the soft muted light filled his bedroom, the last of the nightmare faded from consciousness.

He was here. In bed. Alone. Why had he dreamed about that day again? He hadn't thought about it for such a long time.

He got out of bed, his teeth chattering, and reached for his robe, then sat down in the chair by the window. Staring out into the darkness, he willed himself back under control.

When he finally returned to bed, he looked at the phone for a moment, wishing he had the right to call her. Wishing she was in bed with him and he could curl up against her and hold her in his arms.

Wishing he wasn't so alone.

"I'VE GOT it!" Anne whispered the next morning as she closed the dressing-room door. She handed Genie a typewritten photocopied sheet.

"You are terrific." Genie leaned against the back of a chair, resplendent in her black satin dress, as she quickly scanned the list. *Thank God for a photographic memory.* It was one of her biggest assets as an actress, and it would serve her well today. Interesting questions. She smiled slowly as she read over the list one last time. There was nothing Pierce could do to fluster her today.

And she would need the extra edge—though she wouldn't admit to herself what she was beginning to feel for Pierce.

Within the hour she was standing by the closed curtain. As she heard Pierce announce her, it took all the willpower she possessed to become Valerie Bouchet once again.

Give them the fantasy. Taking a deep relaxing breath, she swept out onto the stage, smiling brilliantly. The black satin of her strapless gown picked up the lights and glimmered with reflections as she moved, slowly, seductively, toward Pierce. Her hair had been swept up in a classic chignon, and the diamond earrings were back in place. A matching necklace graced the smooth skin of her throat. She knew skillful makeup hid the results of her sleepless night, so Genie was confident she looked as good as she'd ever looked in her life.

Pierce looked awful, though he was immaculately groomed. Something in his eyes—they were flat and dull, as if he were in pain. Genie immediately noticed the extra bit of stage makeup applied to his face. He looked tired.

Perhaps this series of interviews was beginning to wear on him, too.

Genie knew the first question on the list was going to be difficult. If she and Pierce had remained enemies, battling publicly, it would have been humiliating, amusing, a contest of wills. But too much had happened between them.

No matter how he felt about her, Pierce couldn't deny what had happened in her suite. The attraction between them was simply too volatile.

She knew what the question would cost him, and also knew he would ask it. As Anne had said at lunch, he understood the mind of his audience, and he knew what they wanted to hear.

"Hello, Valerie." A bit of warmth returned to his eyes as he greeted her.

"Hello, Pierce. It's good to see you."

His mouth tightened momentarily, and for a second Genie thought he was going to completely disregard the typewritten sheet in front of him and begin asking her questions that really mattered.

But he didn't. Pierce was nothing if not responsible.

"To satisfy the curiosity of our studio audience—" Genie was glad he prefaced the question so carefully "—which one of your erotic scenes do you think captures what you'd like your dream lover to do to you?"

There was a delighted gasp from the audience. *Sex sells,* Genie thought. She smiled seductively, knowing she had to convincingly portray her sister's image. "I'd have to say the scene from my third novel, *Fast Lane.*"

"And which scene is that?" There was something in his expression telling her he wished he didn't have to be here, with her, on public display.

But better in public than in private. When they were alone together, her emotions were too dangerous.

"In the last half of the book, Steve comes to Michelle's apartment to confront her about the depth of his feeling for her. She hasn't wanted an involvement with him because—" Genie faltered for just an instant, then regained control "—because she's married to another man. But Steve, in true heroic style, won't take no for an answer." Nervously she wet her lips. "He asks her how she can deny the feelings between them." Not daring to look at Pierce, she finished her answer to his question as quickly as she could. "So in order to get her past the point of caring, he makes passionate love to her."

When she finished, the studio audience clapped and cheered, obviously pleased with what had been revealed about Genie. Genie slowly raised her eyes to Pierce's, and the expression she caught tore at her heart.

He cares.

THE PHONE WAS RINGING as Genie returned to her suite, and she rushed toward it, the black satin swishing around her legs.

"Hello?" Her voice was breathy. She thought it might be Pierce.

"Genie, what the hell is going on out there?" Al's voice was filled with concern. "I just finished watching the show. What's with you and Stanton?"

As much as she loved Al, she couldn't talk about her feelings for Pierce. They were too new. Too tender. "Nothing."

"But it looks like the two of you—Genie, I've never seen him like this."

"What do you mean?" she asked, her heart beginning to race. If it was apparent to Al on television, maybe the look she'd seen in his eyes hadn't been her imagination.

"He's fascinated with you. He looks like he wants to carry you offstage and ravish you. Am I making myself clear?"

Dear Al. "Remember when I told you something didn't seem right?" Glancing quickly at the clock on the fireplace mantel, Genie realized Al was spending considerable money to call her in the middle of the day. "Let me phone you back and bill it to Valerie."

She called and quickly explained about her sister's involvement with Pierce's family.

He whistled softly. "So you had an affair with his brother-in-law and destroyed his family's honor!"

"It was a real mess. I don't know how Val could have let me walk into this."

"I do." The note in his voice was grim. "Genie, I want you to be careful. Do you know anything about Pierce's family?"

"Should I?"

"There was no such thing as divorce in the Stanton family—until Robert Tyler."

"How do you know?"

"I read an article in some magazine last month."

"Oh, my God! No wonder he was so angry with me."

She could hear Al's muttered expletives over the phone; then he said, "Listen, you have one more interview to get through. Just make it through the taping and catch the first plane out of there."

After she hung up the phone, Genie sat back in her chair and slowly pleated the heavy black satin of her skirt between her fingers.

Everything Al had said made perfect sense. The only question was, did she want to follow the logic of her mind—or the instincts of her heart?

Chapter Five

Unable to settle down that evening, Genie prowled around her suite, pacing restlessly back and forth across the large living room.

I have to get out of here. Anything was better than being alone with her thoughts.

Racing to her bedroom, she grabbed her short mink jacket and threw it on over gray flannel pants and a cowl-necked silk sweater in variegated shades of mauve and lavender.

The hotel lobby was almost deserted. Most of the guests were probably eating dinner in one of the many restaurants. Realizing she was hungry, Genie headed into the small gift shop and bought a chocolate bar. She was leafing through a fat paperback novel when a familiar low voice caught her ear.

''Checking up on the competition?''

She looked up to find Pierce studying her and almost dropped the book. In her room upstairs she had washed off the masklike heavy studio makeup she usually wore. Her hair was free from the confines of the sophisticated chignon, falling over her shoulders and down her back like a silken black waterfall.

She knew she looked more like Genie than Valerie tonight.

He noticed the change. "You look different tonight."

"I...thank you."

Was it her imagination, or did he seem as uneasy as she felt?

"I was wondering if...you'd like to have dinner with me again."

His question hung in the air as Genie thought quickly. She wanted to be with Pierce, she had no doubts about that. And as long as they stayed in a public place...

"I'd love to." She returned the book to its place on the rack, then looked up into his eyes.

Pierce smiled slowly, and this time the smile reached his eyes. "Let's go." He extended his hand and she took it, feeling the gentle pressure as his fingers laced with hers. His facial features had softened in a way Genie was coming to know. And dread. It weakened her resistance.

She made a quick decision. Tonight was a gift she was going to give herself. Tonight she would be Genie, not Val, and pretend she had met Pierce herself. Genie knew she could only have memories of this man, and she decided they'd be happy ones.

They walked down Michigan Avenue, looking in store windows, talking about anything and everything. A guarded intimacy began to unfold between them. Genie was determined to know Pierce the man, not Pierce Stanton, talk-show host. And he seemed just as determined to avoid controversial subjects and enjoy their evening together.

He took her to a small coffee shop. Again, it was

not a place she thought he would normally frequent. But the food was excellent and unpretentious. They concluded their meal with coffee and thick slices of coconut cream pie.

Pierce signaled for their waitress to refresh his cup of coffee. "You seem more relaxed tonight. There's something new about you...."

Genie didn't want him to think about her transformation. She still couldn't afford to destroy her cover. "I think I'm just finally relaxing. I was a little scared coming to a strange city. And," she said demurely, not being able to resist a chance to tease, "it's a lot easier when we're not arguing on the air."

He grinned. "You managed to hold your own." In seconds his expression changed, and Genie realized with a thrill that he was concerned for her. "Did I upset you today?" She knew her answer was important to him.

"Describing my ultimate sexual fantasy on nationwide television?" She sat back in her seat. "No. I knew you did it for the audience. Were you upset?"

He paused, and Genie was worried for a second before she realized he was teasing her, too, using the time for dramatic effect. "Let's just say it was a unique experience."

Looking at him sitting across the small table, Genie suddenly wished with all her heart that she'd met Pierce in different circumstances. Why couldn't they have had a chance to really get to know each other? She knew that had fate been kinder, she would have liked him right from the beginning.

What would he think of her if he knew of her deception? The question bothered her as she watched him pay the bill; then she followed him outside into the dark, crisp evening.

"They'll be putting up Christmas lights on Michigan Avenue soon," Pierce mused, tucking her hand into his arm.

"I've seen pictures of it. The trees look magical."

"They do."

Her fantasy evening was coming to an end. But instead of leaving a glass slipper, instead of there being any hope she would see him again, Genie knew she would simply fly home tomorrow, straight out of Pierce's life forever.

And she still knew so little about this man she was coming to care for so deeply.

"Look." He stopped, then tilted her face upward with a gentle hand.

"What?" She didn't know what he was talking about, but she liked the feel of standing close to him, the scent of his citrus cologne, the slight roughness of his topcoat.

"It's starting to snow."

As the first few flakes came down, illuminated by streetlights, Genie stood perfectly still, then stuck out her tongue and caught one in her mouth.

"That's what I love about you," Pierce whispered against her ear, and she thought her heart might stop at the perfection of the moment.

"What?" Her voice shook slightly.

"The enthusiasm you give over to life. The way you meet it head on, with all the energy and passion you're capable of." He searched her face, his blue eyes penetrating. "Have you ever been scared of anything in your life, Valerie?"

She couldn't seem to control her thoughts, couldn't keep from speaking them out loud.

"You," she breathed out, moving slightly closer to his touch. "The way I feel about you frightens the hell out of me." She tilted her head up, wanting him to kiss her, knowing if she kept herself close to him he wouldn't be able to hold out much longer.

"Valerie." It was more a groan than a coherent word. He slowly lowered his mouth to hers.

She could still taste the coffee on his lips as he opened her mouth and probed gently with his tongue. She caught his shoulders with her hands, suddenly needing his support as a delicious weakness invaded her body. Pushing her fingers up into his thick hair, she urged him closer, then sighed as he broke the kiss and moved his lips over her neck and down to the base of her throat.

Only a pedestrian bumping gently against her shoulder made Genie realize where she was and what she was doing. Snow was beginning to fall rapidly, and there was a light dusting on their shoulders and in their hair.

"Let's walk for a while," Pierce said.

Genie barely noticed her surroundings. She was too busy watching Pierce, trying to memorize the man, keep a part of him close to her heart. The way the evening breeze off the lake ruffled his dark hair, his long, athletic stride, the hard warmth of his fingers as they closed around her own.

And tomorrow night she'd be at O'Hare Airport, waiting for her flight to New York and a life that seemed suddenly empty. Genie felt as if she'd finally met her soul mate, someone who understood the way she wanted to live her life—only to lose him.

She made up her mind in that instant. Perhaps the fates wouldn't be too angry if she asked for one night. A night of love with a man whose mere presence ignited a fire within her soul.

But she couldn't rush things.

"Where do you live?" she asked, not knowing what else to say.

"In Evanston. It's only a fifteen-minute drive into the city, but it's like going back to the country every evening." He paused for a fraction of a second. "I'd like to take you there."

It was madness. It wasn't safe. Yet Genie knew she wanted to see Pierce's house, wanted to know how he lived. She didn't want to play it safe and keep herself in a cocoon of careful control. There were no rules when feelings this strong were concerned.

She squeezed his arm gently. "Okay."

She was anxious to preserve this fragile feeling of intimacy and understanding between them, so she didn't say a word as he drove out of the city. The highway took them along the lakeshore, Pierce's Mercedes humming softly. Genie settled back against the soft leather seat and tried to still her racing heartbeat. She swallowed against the dryness in her throat. What would happen when they reached his house?

Within a short time Pierce pulled into the driveway of an enormous gray stone house. Ivy trailed over the façade and immense oak trees dominated the front lawn. There was a welcoming light above the massive wooden door.

Pierce helped her out of the car, and Genie stepped gingerly onto the cobbled driveway. She stared at the size of the house—the closest she had ever been to a place like this was admiring pictures in *Architectural*

Digest. It was like something out of one of Val's novels. Large and imposing. Sensible. Solid. Reliable. Much like the man who lived there.

"Do you like it?"

She wondered why her feelings were important to him. Nodding her head, she turned toward him and smiled reassuringly, though she felt as if she needed reassurance. "It has a lot of character. I've always loved older houses, and this one looks like it's been here awhile."

"It belonged to my mother." He looked away from her, toward the dark stone walls thrown into relief by the light over the door. "She left it to me when she died."

As Pierce opened the front door, two large golden retrievers bounded outside, jumping up and trying to lick his face.

"Down!" They obeyed their master immediately, but their sleek golden bodies quivered with excitement.

"Valerie, meet Jaime and Parrish." His introduction was touchingly formal, and all of a sudden Genie wondered what he had been like as a small boy. Always this reserved? Had he ever really laughed and played?

"How do you do?" she asked gravely. Parrish, the smaller of the two, began to crawl over to her on his belly, as if by doing this he wouldn't be noticed by Pierce. Genie snapped her fingers and suddenly had both dogs snuggling under her hands, weaving around her legs, anxious to be petted. They were like small children let out for recess after hours in the classroom.

"You're not afraid of animals?" Pierce sounded delighted.

She laughed as Jaime tripped over Parrish in an attempt to sniff the hem of her pant leg. "I love them. These two are big clumsy babies."

He seemed pleased.

The inside of Pierce's house was as impressive as its exterior. Rich paneled walls, Oriental carpets and lovingly maintained antiques graced most of the rooms.

Such a silent house, thought Genie as she followed him. Thinking of Pierce living here all alone depressed her.

After giving her a quick tour of the first floor, Pierce built a fire in the den and made Irish coffee.

Sitting in one of the leather chairs by the fire, Genie took a tentative sip from her mug. It was warming and rich. She let the flavors play over her tongue, content simply to enjoy this evening. Setting her coffee down on the antique table in front of them, she glanced at Pierce. He was seated across from her, but his face was in profile, starkly handsome as he stared into the fire.

"You love this house very much, don't you?"

He nodded. "I think of it as a balance to all the confusion at the studio."

"Do you like your job?" It had sounded as if he didn't.

Pierce sighed wearily, running his long fingers through his hair. One lock fell over his forehead, and Genie had to resist the urge to get up and smooth it back, soothe the tension lines from his forehead.

"I've been interviewing people for close to three years now. The show has good ratings, it pays well—people assume I'm on top of the world. But every once in a while, I feel—" He stopped, took a sip of his coffee, set the mug down.

"Go on, Pierce." She wanted to know more about this man. It was her turn to ask the questions.

"I feel as if what I do with my life is essentially pointless." He leaned forward in his chair, his hands loosely clasped, then raised his eyes to hers. "I've never felt it as strongly as...when you came on the show."

"Me?" Genie hadn't suspected he felt this way before tonight.

"Yes. Listening to those women on the phone and in the audience. Valerie, you've affected people's *lives.* I've simply entertained them for a few hours."

"You sell yourself short," she replied softly.

"I don't think so."

They were silent for a time, the only sound the crackling of the fire and the even breathing of the dogs as they lay stretched out on the carpet. Genie closed her eyes, let the heat wash over her body and relax her.

The realization that there was no place she'd rather be came slowly, and she opened her eyes and looked at Pierce. He was watching her, his blue eyes intense, alive with feeling. She looked away, confused. Her emotions had sneaked up on her when she hadn't even been aware.

She cared for him. His hurt was hers. Genie knew what it was to drift, to be unsure of what you wanted. She also knew her work added a special dimension to her life.

She almost closed her eyes again, not wanting to admit what was happening to her, but Pierce spoke softly and she had to look at him.

"I tried to humiliate you. And I've always despised men who mistreat women."

"I'm strong. I didn't break."

He looked at her then, studying her face intently. "You're so different with me tonight. Which woman is really you?"

"This one." She wanted to be close to him. Genie got up from her chair and walked over to Pierce. Leaning over, she brushed her lips softly against his. He didn't respond but pulled back slightly. He stared at her, his eyes dark and troubled.

"I'd better take you back."

THE DRIVE TO HER HOTEL was accomplished in total silence. In the elevator, gliding smoothly up to the twenty-fifth floor, Genie wondered if she'd have the courage to take what she wanted.

Outside her door she tilted her face up to his, studied Pierce's eyes. He looked away. There had been just enough uncertainty in his gaze. Perhaps…

"Pierce?"

"Hmmm?" He sounded distracted, as if he were trying to keep his mind on other things.

"I don't want you to go home."

He turned toward her slowly, and she saw his expression was questioning.

"I want you to stay here with me and—" Her voice caught, and she stopped talking, then swallowed. She'd never tried to seduce a man before. Genie pushed the words through her suddenly dry mouth.

"I want you to make love to me."

Something flared in his eyes, only to be quickly replaced by the bland mask she knew too well. He was trying to push her away.

"I don't think so, Valerie." There was a husky

catch to his voice. "Married women are off limits for me."

"But I'm not married!" The words were out before she could stop them.

He stared at her, astonished.

At that moment, Genie wanted to blurt out the entire truth. But sanity returned, and she remembered she still had one day of taping left. Her job wasn't over yet.

"What I meant is, I don't feel as if I'm married when I feel this way about you." She had to be as honest as she could with him. She touched his arm gently.

"No." It was a sound of pure anguish, torn from his throat. "Give me your key."

She watched him as he unlocked her door, turned on the light and handed the key back, careful not touch her. "Please, Genie, go inside and forget you ever said anything to me."

"No." She was against his body in two steps, then quickly wrapped her arms around him, pressing her cheek against his chest. His heart was pounding furiously. "Pierce, I've never felt about anyone the way I feel about you," she whispered through her tight throat. "And I know you feel it, too! I can sense it in the way you look at me, the way you touch me—"

"No, Valerie." He began to loosen her grip gently, then grasped both her hands in his. "Don't do this."

She broke away from him, stumbling into her room. Her hands fell limply against her sides. What a fiasco she'd made of her feelings. What should have been beautiful was turning into a sordid mess. Why couldn't she have met him another way? Why did Valerie's shadow have to stand between them? Genie had never felt this passionately about anyone so quickly. And she knew she'd have to leave Pierce within days. The knowledge brought a fresh spasm of pain and she bit her lip, hot tears beginning to roll down her cheeks. Powerless to control them, she let her despair sweep over her. Her shoulders shook as she gave way to turbulent emotion, then walked blindly to the sofa and sat down, covering her face with her hands.

"Darling." He was beside her in an instant, cradling her in his arms, rocking her gently. The warmth and strength of his body soothed her, but still she cried as if her heart were breaking.

Her voice shook violently as she tried to force the words out between chattering teeth. "I...want to be with you so much...it hurts! I've never felt this way about *anyone,* and then you throw it back in my face...."

"No. *No.* I care a great deal for you." His voice was harsh. "But if I made love to you once, I'd want you for all time, and we both know that can never happen."

Genie dried her eyes on her sweater sleeve awkwardly, then smiled shakily as Pierce pushed a square of linen into her fingers.

"Blow."

She didn't know what to do after she'd used his handkerchief, so she held it in a tightly crumpled ball in her fist.

She couldn't even look at him. Genie hadn't meant to manipulate him with tears—her feelings had simply exploded out of her. Now, embarrassed, she studied the pattern of the carpet. What could she say to Pierce to make things better?

His voice was so soft she thought she was imagining it when he began to speak.

"I haven't been completely honest with you. I've been attracted to you from the beginning. The first day I saw you in the dressing room." He laughed self-consciously. "I wouldn't call it love, what you did to my blood pressure, but I was definitely interested. But then day after day, as you answered my questions with such passion, I grew to respect you. That night we quarreled and I kissed you—I went home and called myself all sorts of names. As much as I blamed my brother-in-law for betraying Barbara, how could I judge him when I wanted you in the worst possible way? And knowing you have a husband."

"Pierce—"

"Wait. I told myself I kissed you because I wanted to hurt you, to humiliate you." He took a deep breath. "But I was lying to myself. I'm very good at that. Those heroes you write about, the ones who have their feelings at their fingertips?"

She could feel tears starting again. "Don't."

"There are times when I'm not even sure I know what I'm feeling. Half my job at the studio is to keep myself so busy I won't think about what's lacking in my life." He clenched his hands into fists. "I didn't even think much about feelings. Until you came into my life."

The room was so quiet she could hear his harsh breathing.

"I'd die for a chance to spend my nights in your arms."

She bent her head, fresh tears beginning to spill out of her eyes.

"All I know," said Pierce in a roughly emotional

voice, "is that I'm going to have to watch you walk out of my life and feel my insides being ripped apart. You brought me everything. With you, there's feeling and warmth—I wanted to kidnap you tonight, hide you at my house. I've sat up the past few nights and pictured you lying in my bed at night, thought about waking up next to you in the morning."

"Oh, God," she whispered brokenly. Why had she ever agreed to Valerie's deception?

"I've never felt this way about any woman but you." He stood up, walked carefully to the door and opened it.

She watched him leave through her tears, feeling as if she were dying inside.

PIERCE WALKED SLOWLY down the hotel hall, the set of his shoulders revealing his defeat. He was glad Valerie couldn't see him, didn't know what it had cost him to leave her room.

You have to be stronger. It was a dangerous game he was playing—dangerous because he couldn't seem to control his attraction to Valerie. Of all the women he'd known, she alone remained an enigma. Fascinating. It was almost as if she were two women: the sensuous author and the woman he'd seen tonight. Her face had been softer. With her hair down her back, she'd looked about ten years younger. Yet the two women were contained in one body flawlessly.

And the woman who had responded to him tonight was another facet of Valerie. He would have expected her to be slightly jaded having supposedly done and seen everything. She ran with a crowd where sex was simply another commodity.

But her emotions had come straight from her heart.

No one could have faked tears like that. They'd come from deep within, shaking her body and making her tremble.

And no one could have faked how she'd responded sexually. The way she'd kissed back, wrapped her arms around him. If he'd been told Valerie was going to do this to him, he would have suspected something behind it. Cool, deliberate calculation. But this woman couldn't manipulate someone if her life depended on it.

He wondered what she would have been like on the show if he hadn't ripped into her from the beginning. He'd insisted on asking questions that were little more than thinly veiled insults. And she'd held her own. Even made him look like a fool.

He could still remember the startled look in her eyes when he'd shot his first question at her. This was no sophisticated, brittle woman. Perhaps artists had to remain open to their feelings in a way he'd never understand.

But she was breaking into his feelings with a speed that was frightening. He'd never told any woman how he felt about her. With Valerie, the admission had been painful, but he hadn't hesitated letting her know how he felt.

Where do we go from here? There was no easy answer. She was married. He didn't know anything about her relationship with her husband. Did they have an open marriage? His image of Valerie before they'd actually met would have included a totally uncommitted relationship. But not the woman he'd just left.

He continued to think about her as he reached the parking garage and as he drove home to his silent house. It seemed lonely now, without her. He'd never been bothered by solitude before.

All Pierce knew was that she had managed to quietly slide under his defenses. What happened to her mattered to him. He didn't want to fight with her on the show anymore. He didn't particularly care what his audience wanted to hear.

He was going to ask Valerie some of the questions that had been intriguing him since he'd first seen her.

GENIE LAY AWAKE for a long time in the quiet hotel room. As the hours slipped by and the Chicago skyline began to lighten, she realized the futility of trying to sleep. Getting up, she padded over to the window and looked out over the city.

She loved him. She didn't know when or how it had happened, but she loved him. Perhaps it was the vulnerability he'd shown tonight, the way he'd tried to make amends for their disastrous first interview. Or maybe it was the gentleness and consideration she could see beneath the surface when he was relaxed. Or simply the intelligence and humor in his eyes.

When had she started to care so deeply? It was more than sexual, though those feelings burned with a passion that left her shaking. Genie knew she'd started to fall in love with Pierce when he shared his feelings with her. She hadn't liked the arrogant way he handled her the first two days on his show. It had all started when he asked her out the first time. Asked if he could kiss her.

She'd sensed banked fires inside him, and she'd been right. No one had ever kissed her the way he had. No one had ever made her feel so alive. More than anything, she wanted to follow her heart, but she knew eventual disaster lay in taking that course of action.

Turning away from the window, Genie dropped into a chair, tucking her bare legs beneath her. She loved him. And he thought she was Valerie Bouchet.

Though she'd successfully acted the part of a best-selling novelist, Genie knew she'd been herself with Pierce at dinner and later at his home in Evanston. She was frustrated portraying someone she wasn't. It was fine within the confines of an acting assignment, but in real life all it produced was an incredible emotional mix-up.

Since she couldn't sleep she showered, changed into her final costume, and made herself a cup of peppermint tea.

When the limousine arrived, she was already downstairs.

"HERE YOU ARE." Anne handed her the last sheet of questions.

Genie took them, barely glancing at Anne. She didn't like the thought of doing this to Pierce, but her nerves were stretched to the point where she needed an extra edge. No surprises today. She couldn't handle them.

"They're ready for you, Miss Bouchet," the producer said with a smile. Genie automatically smiled back, her most gracious expression. How she'd come to hate her role!

When she heard his voice announcing her, she wanted to sit down and cry. But of course she didn't. A good actress could smile in the face of disaster.

Despite her inner turmoil, Genie turned on a high-voltage smile for the audience as she swept in front of the curtain. The excited exclamations from the audience did little to cheer her inside. Valerie had saved the most elaborate dress for last, a silver sequined sheath that clung to her body, revealing every line of her figure. The dress caught the light, flashed it back as she moved across the stage. Her hair had been left down and flowed behind her like a cape. She took her time walking across the soundstage, making sure the audience had their fill of her last costume before she settled herself in the now familiar chair.

Pierce looked terrible. She was sure he hadn't slept, either. There were faint shadows underneath his eyes even television makeup couldn't conceal, and taut lines were etched around his eyes and mouth. Her heart went out to him.

"Good morning, Pierce."

"Good morning, Valerie."

The feelings left unsaid were eloquently expressed as each looked at the other, concern in their eyes.

Genie tried to make herself comfortable and mentally prepared herself to answer the first question on the list she'd memorized.

He never asked it.

"Valerie, I thought we'd spend the first part of the program talking about the men you write about."

She almost replied with a prepared answer, but years of acting instruction had taught her, above all else, *to listen.* Swallowing against the sudden tightness in her throat, she realized what Pierce was really asking her.

"I think they all possess qualities a woman would like to find in a man."

"What are they?"

Genie was on familiar ground. Ever since Pierce had

begun her interview, she'd felt as if she were in a French farce, with the script supplied courtesy of Valerie. But now her words were spoken from deep feeling.

Remembering their evening together made speaking difficult. "Sensitivity. A sense of humor. A man who's secure enough to feel deeply, to be a complete partner in an emotional relationship." None of the words were rehearsed, they came straight from her heart.

"What else do you like in the men you write about?" It was clear Pierce was getting his answers to these very personal questions.

"Loyalty. A unique outlook on the world. A man who's strong enough to listen to his inner convictions. A man who doesn't resort to violence."

As they neared the end of the hour, Pierce asked her his final question.

"It's said that writers live examined lives—meaning, everything they write helps them understand themselves better."

Go out in a blaze of glory, Genie thought, trying desperately to keep her composure. Would she ever see Pierce again after today?

"What is the most valuable thing you've learned as a writer?"

She cleared her throat, determined not to break down and destroy five days of work. Yet she wanted to make sure Pierce knew how she felt.

"I think if there's one thing I've learned while writing my books, it's that...there really is a tremendous power in simple human emotion. Love can produce miracles; you can see it all the time if you look. I write novels about people and their relationships. The love a mother has for a child, the way a man and a woman will fight unbelievable odds if they really love each other."

She saw his eyes close briefly, his mouth tighten. But she continued. She had to leave a part of herself with him.

"There's always enough love if you open your heart to your true feelings. And deep inside—" She paused, hating the way her voice had grown thick with emotion. "Deep inside, I think everyone wants a chance to have that special love, the love that, when you find it, makes you realize you were sleepwalking your way through life before."

The applause was thunderous, and Genie looked down at her hands, tightly clasped in her lap.

The show was over. Her performance at an end. As Genie sat quietly and smiled for the camera, she wished she'd never agreed to her sister's request. Yet if she'd had the power to look into the future, she still might have taken this job, to meet Pierce. All the pain would have been worth it, knowing she'd found a man this special.

Only to walk straight out of his life forever. How could she have known this job would cost her so much?

Pierce was engulfed by well-wishers—producers, cameramen, technicians. Everyone seemed to want to tell him what a terrific series of interviews he'd managed to pull off. Genie watched him, happy for his success.

No one approached her. It was to be expected. None of the crew really knew her. Valerie had told her many times that people were afraid to approach a bestselling author.

Feeling cold inside, and very tired, Genie retreated

quietly to her dressing room. She picked up her bag and stuffed it full of makeup and brushes, and left the silent cubicle, running swiftly down the hall.

It's better this way. Genie tried to convince herself of this as she climbed into the waiting limousine. She kept her head averted from the studio doors as the car pulled away.

THE PHONE WAS RINGING as she lay in her hotel suite. She picked up the receiver with reluctance. No doubt it was Valerie, wondering what the hell was going on.

"Genie!" Al.

"Al?" Her voice was high-pitched. Tight. Hurting.

"What's going on between you and Stanton?"

"I can't talk about it right now."

"You're in love with him."

She started to cry then, hating her weakness, almost hating Al for being so perceptive when she needed to dull the pain, to block Pierce out of her mind.

"The body language going on between the two of you, the eye contact. Hey, sweetie, don't cry! What's the matter?"

"I love him, and he says he cares for me—"

Al let out a whoop. "Then what's the problem?"

"He still thinks I'm Valerie, and I don't know how to tell him I'm *not!* I'm *me!* But he won't make love to me because he thinks I'm married to Harold—"

"Can't you tell him?"

"How can I? How can I expect him to be thrilled when he finds out one of the best interviews of his career was with an imposter?"

"God, what a mess. The next time Valerie asks you to do anything—"

"Never again." Genie sniffed slightly. "Al, what am I going to do?"

"Are you flying home tonight?"

"I suppose so."

"Why don't you stay one more day? Go talk to Pierce, maybe the two of you can work something out."

"He'll never understand."

"He's human, isn't he? Look, why don't you invite him up to dinner, then after the two of you make love and he's all fuzzy, you can sort of slip him the truth."

She started to laugh, then began to cry again. "I tried to seduce him last night, and he walked out." Her admission was painful, even to a close friend like Al.

"Is he gay?"

"No."

"Listen, why don't you try seducing him the way Valerie would have someone do in one of her books? You can't do it yourself, you're too emotionally messed up right now."

"Al..." Doubt laced her voice.

"Trust me. Think of it as an acting problem." As Al began to outline a plan, Genie brightened. Valerie had gotten her into this mess; maybe indirectly she could get her out. Perhaps Al was right. How mad could Pierce be when he found out she wasn't married?

After she hung up the phone, she stared at it for several seconds. Did she have the right to do this? Would Pierce hate her when he found out about the deception? What was the right thing to do?

I love him. I know he cares. I won't leave Chicago without telling him the truth.

Picking up the receiver, she dialed the studio.

"Yes?" The secretary sounded preoccupied.

"May I speak to Pierce Stanton?"

"Who shall I say is calling?"

"This is... Valerie Bouchet."

"I'll get him for you, Miss Bouchet. I just loved your latest book." And with that she clicked off the line, and Genie waited, her breath held painfully tight.

"Valerie?" Pierce's voice was questioning.

She took a quick breath. "I was wondering if—if you'd care to come by tonight and have dinner with me."

"When do you leave?" he asked quietly.

"Late tonight." Mentally she made a note to change her flight reservation to Saturday afternoon.

He lowered his voice. "You know I'd like to see you. But I think we should avoid being alone."

She crossed her fingers. "Of course."

"What time will you be ready?"

"Is eight too late?"

"Fine. I'll be there. I can take you to the airport afterward."

"I'd like that, Pierce."

Genie raced through the next hours. She called room service and arranged dinner for two—to be delivered fifteen minutes before Pierce's arrival. She tore through the clothes Valerie had picked out for her, trying to decide what she should wear. What did one wear for a seduction?

Finally she settled on a black silk dressing gown, with puffed sleeves and embroidery on the front yoke. Jet beads sparkled among the intricate stitches. Valerie had included it in her wardrobe stating that she needed to immerse herself in the proper image of luxury twenty-four hours a day. Genie smiled as she held up the gown, imagining Pierce's response when he saw it.

As she rummaged through the rest of the silk underwear her sister had purchased, her hands closed around a merrywidow. She held it up and studied it. When worn, the garment pushed up her breasts, nipped in her waist and exposed a terrific expanse of leg.

Genie could still remember Pierce's expression the day he'd walked into her dressing room and found her sitting in her slip.

Why not pull out all the stops? After all, the seduction would be done as Valerie, with the truth to come afterward.

Trying on the garment in the bathroom, Genie had to admit it certainly enhanced her figure. The top pushed her breasts up until an amazing amount of cleavage was exposed. The bottom, adorned with silken ruffles, had garters to hold a pair of French seamed stockings. Her black heels and a silk bikini would complete the outfit.

She took a quick bath in Opium-scented oil, washed her hair under the shower, then blew it dry and brushed it until it gleamed. Dressing carefully, she slipped on a pair of string bikini panties, and then adjusted the hooks on the merrywidow.

Thank God it fastens up the front. It might be a hard garment to get out of, but it made her look so wickedly sensual. She unrolled the silk stockings over her calves and thighs, then fastened them to the garters.

What was it Pierce had said about seeing her the first time? *I wouldn't call it love, what you did to my blood pressure, but I was definitely interested.* She only hoped her outfit would have the same effect on him tonight.

She studied herself with satisfaction in the mirror. *If this doesn't interest him, he's dead below the waist.*

Donning the dressing gown, a swirl of black silk, she belted it tightly around her, then arranged her hair on top of her head with a few strategically placed pins and spayed herself lightly with perfume.

At seven-thirty, Genie waited by the door until she heard the rattle of the food cart. She let the young attendant in and instructed him to wheel the trolley over to the table by the window. He had brought two candles with him as she'd requested. Lighting the white tapers, he set them in the middle of the table, then placed the covered dishes on the snowy linen.

She gave him an overly generous tip and hurried him out the door, after letting him know she wouldn't be needing his services for the remainder of the evening.

When the telephone buzzed, she jumped.

"A Mr. Stanton is on his way to your suite, Miss Bouchet."

"Thank you. I don't want to be disturbed tonight, so I'll take any phone messages in the morning before I check out."

A few minutes later, she heard a knock on the door. She opened it quickly.

Pierce had obviously been expecting to take her out. He looked perfectly at ease in his gray suit and steel-blue shirt. He'd planned something special, just as she had.

Taking a deep breath, she smiled up at Pierce with confidence born of love and her heart in her eyes.

Chapter Six

''Valerie.'' It was all Pierce said. But it was enough. The look he gave her as he took in her silk-clad figure said it all.

Then he looked away. ''I've made reservations for us at—''

''I've made reservations for us right here.'' She touched his arm gently and gestured over to the table.

''No, Valerie. I don't think this is a good idea.''

''Pierce. Please.'' Genie tried to keep her voice from shaking. ''This is the last time I'll ever see you. I don't want to share you with a group of people. I just want to be with you.''

He started to say something else, but she turned and walked toward the table and stared out over Lake Michigan. He didn't want to be alone with her. Biting the inside of her cheek, she willed herself to stay calm.

''It's okay, Pierce. I know you're tired. Take off your jacket and relax.''

There was no sound from him, no movement. He still wasn't convinced.

''I promise you I won't seduce you,'' she said, her fingers crossed within the folds of the dressing gown, a swirl of black silk.

"You wouldn't have to, wearing something like that."

She turned slowly. His blue eyes were serious.

Her plan was working.

She watched him as he took off his suit jacket and placed it carefully on one of the chairs. He rolled up the sleeves of his shirt with precise gestures, then said in a carefully controlled voice, "I guess I'd better get comfortable."

She could barely control the trembling in her stomach. "There's a bathroom down the hall."

As soon as he was out of sight, Genie unbuttoned the top three buttons of her dressing gown. The merrywidow pushed her breasts up, and with the buttons of her gown unfastened, her cleavage was in full view. Pierce would have to be blind to miss it.

He didn't.

As soon as he came back into the room, he saw what she'd done. Pretending not to notice, he took his seat. *The perfect gentleman,* Genie thought with despair. *We'll see.*

She began to dish up bowls of clear consommé. They ate in silence, but Genie noticed Pierce barely touched his food. Neither did she. The candlelight bathed the suite in warm light, the flame flickering over the crystal.

"So you fly out tonight?" Pierce was still attempting to keep their evening strictly platonic.

"Yes," she replied as she raised her wineglass to her lips and took a large swallow. She had the feeling she'd need a little wine to pull this seduction off.

He pushed his half-eaten bowl of soup aside. "What next?"

You. "Filet Mignon. I've heard the meat in Chicago

is terrific.'' She tried to suppress a smile as her over-active imagination conjured up bawdier images.

''Usually.''

She dished up his plate: filet, baked potato, baby peas. As she handed him his food, she was careful to ''accidentally'' brush her fingers against his. She felt them tremble slightly, and Genie realized with sudden clarity that he was just as nervous about tonight as she was.

The knowledge gave her courage. She wasn't alone with her feelings.

Genie waited until he had taken a bite of his filet before she said softly, ''I'll miss you, Pierce.''

He almost choked. Rapidly swallowing, he put his fork down and stared at her. ''Valerie, don't start. I'm not superhuman.''

''Pierce, I'm not—''

''Think of your husband.''

''I've thought of him, yes.''

Pierce's eyes blazed, but Genie sensed his anger wasn't directed at her. ''*Thought* of him! My God, is that the best you can do?''

''Yes.'' She set her wineglass down firmly. ''How can I spend my time thinking about Harold when all I can do is think about you?''

''Valerie, no...'' His words came out a groan.

''I dream about you, Pierce.''

He didn't look her in the eye, directing his gaze slightly to her left. Finally dropping his eyes to his plate, he slowly picked up his knife and fork.

Genie sipped her wine silently. Then, to show him she wasn't nervous, she began to cut her filet into small pieces.

The silence stretched between them until Pierce

asked, ''Just what kind of things do you dream about?''

She half closed her eyes and parted her lips slightly, as she'd been told to do at so many photo sessions. Seductive, the photographer had assured her. Genie paused for dramatic effect. ''I'd like to make love to you tonight. All night.'' Where she acquired her audacity, she didn't know. She only knew she didn't want Pierce to walk out that door tonight.

''Stop.'' Pierce threw down his napkin and pushed back his chair. His voice rasped unevenly as he forced the words out. ''If I make love to you, I'll want you for all time. I won't be able to live on memories. I'll want you in my bed, by my side forever. And you belong to another man.''

''I belong to *me!* My heart's my own to give.'' She pushed her chair back, moved quickly to his side of the table and looped her arms around his neck, settling herself on his lap. ''Pierce, some people wait all their lives to feel what we do for each other. Do you know what *I* think the crime is? Not betraying Harold—which I'm *not.*'' She brushed her lips against his neck, felt his quickly indrawn breath. ''But betraying myself because I'm not doing what I think is right.''

Things were moving along much faster than in the imaginary scenario Genie had run through her head a thousand times since she'd first thought of seducing Pierce. But she had to keep going.

''I've never felt for any other man the way I feel about you. I want to spend the night with you. I want to push myself to my limit, have all of you tonight. No holding back, no thinking of anyone or anything else.''

He sat motionless, his body still frozen away from

hers. Genie snuggled closer, wanting him to respond. Suddenly, with a quickness and ferocity that surprised her, Pierce rose abruptly, dumping her on the carpet.

"No, Valerie. I can't, not after—" He was almost at the door; then his hand grasped the knob.

As Genie stood up, her legs shook so badly she thought she'd collapse. Her heart pounded as if ready to burst from her chest. This wasn't the way she'd envisioned things happening. She had one last gambit, but she hoped she wouldn't have to use it. What if he rejected her, kept going right out that door? What if he thought she was horrible for playing with his masculine appetites?

But all's fair. She did it.

Her shaking fingers working rapidly, she unbuttoned the tiny buttons, slipped the black silk off her shoulders, down her waist, over her thighs, to a pool of silken material at her feet.

"Pierce."

Her urgent voice made him turn. The atmosphere in the room changed with the swiftness of a summer lightning storm. His dark-blue eyes swept over her, taking in the tight fit of the merrywidow, the way the garment lifted and pushed her breasts together, skimmed tightly over her waist and the beginnings of her hips. The way it stopped short in a mass of lace ruffles, then down to garters fastened to silk stockings, then her heels. Then up again, to her face. And in his expression blazed the hottest, most naked passion she'd ever seen in a man's eyes.

Then he moved. One step, two, then quickly he caught her up in his arms, pulling her against his chest. She could feel the rapid pounding of his heart; it seemed a part of her body. His steps were quick and assured as he carried her down the hall. He found the bedroom, kicked the door shut behind them, and deposited her on the bed.

As soon as his arms were free, Pierce reached for the buttons of his shirt, then skimmed it off. He kicked off his shoes as his hands reached for the buckle of his belt.

Within seconds he was naked, on the bed with her, pulling her beneath him. His lips covered hers in a hungry kiss as his hands grasped her hips, pulling her closer.

He set her on fire wherever he touched her. She gave in to pure feeling, letting the instincts of her body dictate what she did. Forgetting everything else but the man beside her, Genie dismissed her inhibitions. She had one night with Pierce. It would be a moment in time she would remember for the rest of her life. Her hands explored the hard muscles of his back, his sides, his chest. There was a desperate urgency in him that matched her own, and she knew she'd been right to fight for this moment. It had been inevitable from the beginning.

Pierce raised his body up on his elbows and looked down at her. His gaze took in her face, her neck, the swell of her breasts.

"Get that thing off. Now."

The tables had been completely turned, roles exchanged. He'd become the seducer, she the seduced.

Her hands shook so badly she couldn't manage. Brushing her fingers aside, he began to unfasten the tiny hooks.

"This thing must have been designed to destroy a man's patience," he said, a half-smile quirking his lips.

He unfastened the garters, then dropped the merrywidow over the side of the king-sized bed. Not stopping to remove her stockings or shoes, he pressed her back against the bed, the warmth of his body melting into hers.

"Tell me more about your fantasies," he murmured thickly as he kissed the back of her neck, then moved his caresses to her throat.

"I—oh, God." She couldn't think when he touched her, could only feel. Though her past experience with men was limited, no one had ever made her feel this intensity.

"Tell me," he whispered softly; then she felt his hand move up her side, to the swell of her breast. Teasing her with his fingers, he stroked the sensitive skin around her breast slowly, moving closer and closer to where she wanted his touch.

Unable to say anything, she put her hand over his and moved it to her breast. Liquid warmth exploded within her as he lightly brushed her nipple with his fingers. She groaned, and her head pressed back into the mattress as sensation claimed her totally.

"Please," she groaned softly.

"Please what?" he said, then closed his lips over the aroused nipple.

Sensation skyrocketed within her. She cupped his firm buttocks, dug her nails into his flesh as she pulled him closer. He slid between her legs and she cradled him in her thighs, feeling his hard arousal.

"Please. Now..." She'd never pleaded for gratification before tonight. She'd never been brought this far this fast.

His hands moved lower, and she felt his long, sensitive fingers brushing the skin of her inner thighs, moving beneath the elastic of her bikini. Skimming it off.

"Yes," she breathed softly. "Oh, God, Pierce."

"Yes?" He moved his hand higher, touching her gently. "You're so warm here."

She dug her nails into his hips as he began to stroke her. "Please," she moaned again, more urgently this time.

"Not yet." He shifted so he held down one of her legs with his body, held the other thigh with his free hand. "I want you to be completely ready for me."

He let her arousal build slowly, silken inch by inch. Her passion burned quickly, soon almost out of control. Her thighs trembled, feeling stretched tighter and tighter, until she cried out and arched her body toward his hand, knowing she had to be touched deeply. Melting inside, her body shattered with pleasure. Tight, pulsating waves of pure sensation washed through her, and the only thing real was the feeling this man gave her.

When her breathing evened, she opened her eyes and looked up at him. His face was inches from hers, and he kissed her gently.

"You're ready now." He smiled down at her tenderly.

"How can you be so…in control?" she asked softly.

"You think so?" He smiled lazily as his hands moved to her thighs, easing them apart. "Watch me."

He entered her slowly, with each silken thrust giving her more of him. She had never been filled as deeply.

"Am I hurting you?" he asked softly, his warm breath tickling her ear.

"No," she breathed. Then she cupped his buttocks in her palms and pulled him completely into her. She stiffened for just an instant, then relaxed, letting her body accept his fully.

He kissed her as he made love to her, murmuring words almost unintelligible in his passion. His lips skimmed over her throat, her cheeks, the tips of her breasts. And still he thrust into her, all his emotion behind their powerful joining.

She met him with a passion of her own, surprised at her body's extreme reaction. Normally she was passive, not daring to acknowledge needs of her own. But this was Pierce. She loved him, she felt she belonged to him this way. They came together hungrily, each recognizing the other half, their most exquisite resting place.

She could hear his deep, labored breathing, feel the pounding of his heart as he thrust one last time, the deepest possible joining. Then he found release inside her. She held him tightly against her breasts as he cried out, softly, wonderingly, and buried his face in her hair.

They lay together a long time, neither moving. Genie loved the feel of him, a part of her, the weight of his body exciting. She felt fluid and whole, alive and sensitive. When Pierce finally moved, just enough to roll on his side, he caught her hips and took her with him. She groaned, but he silenced her with a kiss.

When she looked up into his eyes, he was regarding her with a warm, searching look. His expression was relaxed, his blue eyes clear. For the first time Genie sensed she had a glimpse of the man within, without defense. It seemed she was too full of emotion, yet at the same time completely at ease, warm and relaxed against his body. She knew it was the same for him. Nothing had to be said. What they had given each other was beyond words.

She felt his lips gently trace her cheek, her temple. "Go to sleep." His voice was a husky murmur. "I'll be here when you wake up."

GENIE OPENED HER EYES slowly, blinking to clear the sleep from them. Pierce was lying alongside her on the bed, his hand spread out on her abdomen. She tried to sit up, but he held her back.

"What are you doing?" she asked. It was exciting being held captive by Pierce.

"I'm going to ravish you until you're speechless." He grinned, his face relaxed and open, then he covered her mouth with his, easing her lips apart and darting his tongue inside. Her stomach contracted wildly as she felt him glide his hand over her hip.

She was shaking when he broke the kiss.

"I just want to make love to you all night long." Taking his hand away, he positioned his hips above hers. The full weight of his aroused masculinity pressed against her stomach and he kissed her neck. "I won't make you wait this time. I want you as badly as you want me." He bit her earlobe, then captured her mouth.

His whispers only excited her more. Yet Pierce took his time, giving her light kisses up and down the length of her arms, over her breasts and her hips, down her legs. There was no part of her body he left untouched while he continued his slow, easy exploration.

As he slid back up her thighs, his warm lips wreaking havoc with her emotions, she gasped.

"I can't take—" She lowered her head and moaned

as he kissed her stomach, then moved lower, building her response with his fingers and tongue. Slowly, tormentingly, Pierce drew out each sensation as much as possible.

Her legs quivered, her body burned. She sucked her lower lip into her mouth, surprised at its tenderness. Biting down, she groaned deep in her throat as she moved closer and closer to fulfillment

He was with her each step of the way until finally she arched her body and cried out, liquid fire blazing through her, exploding where his mouth touched her. This was the strongest sensation she'd ever experienced. She couldn't control it, could do nothing but let go and give in to delicious molten waves of pleasure.

She was panting slightly as he eased his body on top of hers and looked down into her flushed, damp face. Trembling underneath his gaze, she lowered her eyes, suddenly shy.

He moved his body slightly and entered her then, moved slowly within her. She sighed, then kissed the side of his neck, wanting to enjoy each moment they were together.

Moving gently beneath him, matching his rhythm, she was pliable fire in his arms. She felt his fingers cup her face; then he was looking into her eyes as he moved.

She'd never seen a man's face at this intense a moment. But she wanted to remember Pierce the rest of her life. She arched her head slightly, inviting the possession of his lips. He came to her, softly, gently, never breaking the steady rhythm his hips were creating. He kissed her deeply, hungrily. She responded, teasing his mouth with the tip of her tongue.

She felt Pierce tense slightly, but still he kept control, keeping his lovemaking at an intense, steady rhythm. She loved the feel of his flat stomach, his muscular thighs, his hard body pressed against hers.

He reached down and cupped her buttocks, pulling her to him as he began to thrust sharply, began the final climb. She cried out his name at the end as sensations so intense she thought she might die flooded her body. Her excitement was all he needed, and she felt him find his pleasure deep within the softness of her body.

They lay still for a long time, the only sound in the quiet bedroom their rapid breathing. After several minutes, Pierce raised his head, kissed her gently.

"Happy?" His voice was a husky whisper.

She sighed and snuggled against him. "I'd like to show you how happy I am." She wrapped her legs around his body, melting against his hard frame in total surrender.

Later, she traced the hard line of his cheekbone with her fingertip. "It's never been like this for me," she admitted.

He said precisely what she wanted to hear. "Me, too." Then he took her hand, kissing each of her fingertips.

"I could make love to you for the rest of my life," she whispered, biting his ear gently.

He tensed slightly, then rolled over, pulling her on top of him. "Let's not talk about it right now."

THEY MADE LOVE AGAIN. And again. The last time, Pierce was almost frightening in his intensity. It was as if he wanted to mark her as his. Genie met him with a fierce passion of her own. Nothing mattered beyond being in his arms.

She woke as she felt the mattress dip slightly. Raising herself up on one elbow, she was surprised to see Pierce completely dressed, sitting on the edge of the bed putting on his shoes.

''Pierce?'' Her voice was soft with sleep.

He looked over at her. With an expression of infinite tenderness on his face, he reached out and slowly stroked her long dark hair back from her face, then touched her cheek lightly.

''You've given me everything,'' he said softly.

Tell him now, she thought.

''Pierce, I—''

He put a finger to her lips and leaned over to kiss her, their lips touching briefly. ''I'll never forget last night. I've always thought of myself as—cold. I've never been with any woman the way I was with you. I can never give you the smallest amount of what you've given me.''

''But, Pierce, I'm not—''

He silenced her with another kiss, and she felt herself go all warm and weak inside.

''Valerie, some people never experience what we had. I'll carry it with me for the rest of my life.'' He was already distancing himself from her. He stood up and began to walk toward the door. But his back was strangely rigid, and with a flash of insight Genie realized he was in pain.

Because he was leaving her.

''Pierce!'' She was up on her feet in a flash, following him into the living room, her long hair streaming out over her bare shoulders and breasts. Picking up the dressing gown from where she'd left it on the floor, she quickly put it on and belted it around her waist. Then she flew into his arms and held him tightly. It didn't seem possible he was the same man who had made such passionate love to her last night.

And now he was leaving.

"No, Valerie." His voice was low.

"Pierce." Her throat was closing, and tears began to spill down her cheeks. At the moment when she should have told him everything, she was suddenly frightened of his reaction to finding out she was an imposter.

He eased her away from him gently. "We both knew this was the way it would end. We knew going into it. Please, Valerie."

Numbly, Genie stepped back as he opened the door.

He stood looking out into the hallway for a second, then turned to her, pressed his palm against her back as he lifted her up, hard against him. Lowering his head, he kissed her with a sweetness that made her feel her soul was shattering. He kept his hands carefully at the small of her back, but they trembled, and she knew he would need only the slightest amount of encouragement to blaze into passion.

But he broke away, his breathing coming in short, uneven gasps.

"No, Valerie." Without another word, he turned, then stepped out into the hall and began to walk away rapidly.

She stared after him as if she couldn't believe what was happening. *Going. Pierce was going.* She stood by the door as if in a trance until she began to shiver and realized she was standing in the doorway with only a thin silk wrapper covering her cold body. Hugging her arms tightly around her, she shut the door, then dropped down on to the floor and began to cry.

He was gone.

THE MINUTE THE DOOR CLOSED to Valerie's suite, Pierce knew he'd done the wrong thing. But he kept walking, forced his feet to move.

He had to get away.

Inside his car he clutched the steering wheel with tense fingers and stared blindly out the windshield.

You're afraid of the way she makes you feel.

He'd never been as open with a woman. There had never been that loss of control. He'd always managed to hold a part of himself back, keep his emotions in check.

Not this time. He had known it was all the time he'd ever have with her and he wanted it to be different. With nothing to lose, nothing to look forward to after his one night with Valerie, he had let all his barriers down.

It was a shaky feeling. He wasn't sure he liked it. He hadn't been this open emotionally in a long time, not since—

He reached for the ignition. Though emotion flooded his body, urging him to jump out of the car and run back to Valerie, he slowly turned the key and started the engine.

What had she been trying to tell him in the end? That she was willing to leave her husband? Wanted to stay with him? *You're living in a total fantasy if you believe that one.* Valerie belonged to New York, to her penthouse apartment and elegant parties. To Harold Jameson.

As he pulled out of the parking space, he could feel

his emotions being replaced by the iron control he'd lived with for so long.

It's better this way. Better to leave before you get left. Valerie couldn't have stayed with him forever. She had another life in New York. It didn't seem possible he'd only first met her Monday morning. So much had happened to him. He felt as if his life had been sped up and put sharply into focus.

And he didn't like what he was beginning to see.

Chapter Seven

The flight back to New York was depressing. First class was empty, so Genie stretched out over three seats and lay down. She wanted sleep to come and dull some of the pain.

She lay quietly, the plane's vibration all around her. Since her night with Pierce, it seemed she was more open and vulnerable to sensation—the motion of the plane almost made her ill. She closed her eyes, feigning sleep when the flight attendant came by.

Halfway through the short flight, Genie accepted every glass of champagne offered her, so by the time she walked off the plane and into the airport, she was completely smashed.

"Hey, Genie! Over here!" It was Al, looking thinner than when she'd left.

She ran to him and he embraced her. His warm, comforting arms were her undoing, and she started to sob.

"Hey, Genie." He tightened his hold around her shoulders, the bunch of daisies he'd brought her crushed between their bodies. "Hey, take it easy." He patted the back of her head soothingly. "Let's go home, okay?"

"SO HOW COME you couldn't tell him?" Al asked as he poured her a cup of warm milk and brought it to the kitchen table.

"I don't know. There just never seemed to be a perfect time. And then when he was leaving, I was so crazed I didn't know what I was doing."

"The grand passion, huh?"

She nodded, her eyes filling again. She looked away.

"Why can't you phone him? Genie, he'll be thrilled to know you're not married. He'll probably fly right out the same day."

She took a sip of her milk. "You think so?"

"I *know* so. Now drink your milk and get to bed. Your agent left a message on your machine; she wants you to call her Monday morning. You have to be in good shape in case she wants to send you on an interview or something."

She smiled shakily. Dear Al, always so practical. He was right—she was back in her old life now, the job was over, and she needed to be ready for another.

But there was one thing she wanted to do before she slept. "Will you help me with something, Al?"

"Anything."

"Cut my hair."

He stared at her as if she'd gone out of her mind. "Are you crazy? Why?"

Genie spoke slowly, trying to put difficult feelings into words. "All my life I've tried to be like Valerie. This last week...did something to me. I don't want to be like her, I don't want to do anything else for her. I don't even want to look like her! I've always worn my hair this way—" she gestured toward the center part, the long straight hair that reached below her waist "—because *she* wore her hair this way!"

"Why tonight?" Al pleaded. "Why don't you go to a salon on Monday?"

"They'll charge me more if they have to cut if all off. I'll make an appointment, but I want them to trim the ends, not take it off."

"Genie—"

"If you don't do it, I will." She walked into the bathroom and opened a drawer built into the wall, pulling out a pair of hair scissors. "Are you going to?"

Al knew when he was beaten. "Yeah."

She stood very still as he cut, hearing the snip of the scissors, feeling the hair fall. Even before he was done, she felt lighter. All that hair, carried around for so many years. She wanted to leave her past behind.

"You realize you'll have to get new pictures this week," he remarked.

"Big deal. You forget I now have tons of money."

When he finished, she went into the bathroom and studied her reflection.

Not bad. Her hair came to just below her shoulders. Genie was surprised at the natural wave, the new body. All that hair must have pulled it down.

"I love it," she said firmly, then turned and hugged Al. He handed her the scissors.

"I was scared out of my mind the entire time, but I have to admit it doesn't look bad."

She pulled her hair back with her hands and examined the ragged ends. "You're not going to put Vidal Sassoon out of business, but at least most of the work is done. I'll get it recut on Monday."

"I don't think your agent would appreciate your

walking into an audition looking like the bride of Frankenstein." He glanced at his watch. "I'm leaving. Call me tomorrow night, okay?"

"Thanks for doing it, Al."

"Any time, Genie."

After taking a quick shower, she unpacked the clothing Valerie had bought her and pushed it all to the back of her closet.

Time. I just need a little time, that's all.

But Genie lay awake in her loft bed, remembering her night with Pierce. Somehow, though it was less than twenty-four hours ago, it seemed like a lifetime since she'd seen him. Was it possible to miss someone this much? She wondered what he was doing on a Saturday night. Probably sitting in his den, with his dogs, looking at the fire. Had he brought lots of women to his house? Would he find a replacement for her quickly? Deep inside, Genie knew Pierce had been touched as deeply as she by their affair. He didn't deserve the thoughts she was thinking.

She couldn't bear the idea of him with anyone else.

Wearily she rolled over and studied the one brick wall in her studio. The contrast between her studio and her suite in Chicago was depressing. The small loft bed she lay in was nothing like the king-sized bed she'd shared with Pierce. Except for the soreness between her legs and the tenderness of her breasts, she might have dreamed the entire evening.

And if I told him? Genie wondered what he'd think of her. Would he see her as a person who had enjoyed the deceit? Or would he understand what had made her agree to do the show for Valerie?

And Valerie? She wanted Genie to come for lunch

on Sunday. The last person Genie wanted to see. But she had to go. She had to tie up the entire affair.

She rolled over on her stomach and tried not to think of Pierce. *I'll go see Val, and then this whole thing will be over. Forever.*

Somehow, the thought didn't give her any comfort.

"DARLING, you were marvelous!" Valerie moved quickly around the kitchen in her Upper East Side penthouse, dishing out quiche, fruit salad, a pasta dish. It could have been ground glass for all the enjoyment Genie was getting out of it.

As her older sister set down a plate in front of her, Genie automatically picked up her fork. If there was one thing she didn't want, it was Valerie prying into her affairs. Everything had to appear normal. To the end, Genie had applied twice the amount of makeup she normally wore: tons of undereye concealer, a matte foundation and plenty of blusher and eye makeup. She wore her hair in a bun so Valerie couldn't comment on the sudden change in length. The pale face she'd barely recognized as her own in the bathroom mirror this morning had shocked her. Even Chaplin's antics at breakfast couldn't seem to make her laugh.

"I watched every one of your shows—that Pierce Stanton is a *very* handsome man." Valerie laughed throatily as she cut a small piece of quiche for herself. "Maybe I should have done the show after all."

Genie still wanted answers. "Val, did you know how Pierce felt about you for having an affair with his brother-in-law? Is that why you sent me to do the show?"

Valerie nervously toyed with her fork, pushing the

quiche around her china plate. Harold had taken the poodle for a walk, so she was able to talk freely.

"I didn't know he'd be bitter," Valerie conceded.

Genie set down her fork. "*Bitter?* Val, you destroyed a *marriage!* Pierce wasn't bitter over what happened to Robert, but about the way it affected his sister."

"Maybe I used the wrong word. But I don't understand why that man had to take it upon himself to make sure I was punished." She set her fork down and reached for her glass of Perrier. "Anyway, darling, you did a terrific job. You saved my career and my baby, and I'm going to dedicate my next novel to you." It was obvious from the dismissive tone in her voice that Val thought everything had turned out just fine.

Great, thought Genie. "Do you ever think about other people when you plan these little escapades of yours?"

"Why, Genie, whatever are you talking about?"

"When you had your affair with Robert, when you sent me to Chicago to do your dirty work—"

"You were well paid, Genie. You chose to take the job. Besides, you should be proud of the acting job you did! I saw the way you flirted with Pierce Stanton! You had him eating out of your hand and enjoying every minute of it!"

The conversation was coming too close to what Genie didn't want her sister to suspect. "Forget it, Val."

"I don't understand you, Genie. It was only one week out of your life! Now you have enough money to support yourself for the next six months. You can concentrate on your so-called career without having to worry—" Val broke off in mid-sentence. Her eyes widened, and she put her hand against the swell of her stomach.

"Val?" Genie forgot the slight animosity in her sister's voice immediately. "Is this it?"

Her sister nodded her head. "I think—I've been having back pains all morning. Genie—"

"Sit still, Val. I'll call your doctor." Years of looking after her sister made Genie take over automatically.

Harold returned within minutes, and after some initial pandemonium and a hurried conference with Dr. Stevens, Genie waved her sister and Harold off in a taxi. Harold promised to call her as soon as the baby was born.

Only one week out of your life. Genie thought about what Valerie had said as she walked home. Normally she would have taken a subway, but she wanted to walk. It was her way of clearing her thoughts. The late-afternoon sunshine was pale, and piles of gray snow lined the sidewalk. An occasional bird hopped along on the snow and ice, but the chilly winter streets were nearly deserted.

One week out of your life. It had seemed like a lifetime to Genie. She'd never thought it possible to love so quickly, so passionately. Yet she'd barreled headlong into Pierce's life and traveled the gamut of emotions from hating him to loving him—in less than a week. She'd made passionate love to a man she'd known exactly five days. She'd given him her heart and soul, and when they parted she felt her world was completely torn apart.

The cold wind felt good on her face. She stopped at a café and bought a cappuccino to go, then kept walking. She'd tire herself out so she could sleep properly tonight, then call her agent in the morning. Al was right—she had to be prepared for whatever life might bring her way.

"WOULD YOU LIKE SOME COFFEE, Mr. Stanton?" Anne stuck her head around the door of Pierce's office and smiled.

"No, thank you, Anne, but I appreciate the offer." Pierce didn't look up from his desk as his secretary shut the door quietly behind her.

He was studying the new master list of questions he'd prepared. But he couldn't seem to work up any enthusiasm for his guest. Closing his eyes, he willed himself to concentrate.

When he glanced at the list again, it could have been written in Arabic. He pushed it away with a sigh of disgust. Crossing his arms on top of his desk, he leaned his forehead against them and closed his eyes.

With a fresh burst of pain, he realized he could still smell her cologne on his suit jacket. It seemed that everywhere he looked he was reminded of Valerie—whenever he walked by the hotel, out on the soundstage, by the dressing room. And at home, in his den...

He'd never taken any woman to his house. He hadn't even known why he'd taken Valerie there—just an impulse, and at the time he hadn't looked beneath the surface or questioned his motives. But now, whenever he sat in the den and watched the flames dance, he couldn't help but visualize her sitting in one of the chairs next to him, the dogs lying at her feet.

His life had been adequate until Valerie had entered it.

Pierce slowly reached into the bottom left-hand drawer of his desk and pulled out a photograph that had been taken of the two of them. She'd been wearing the black satin strapless dress and diamond earrings. Her hair had been pulled off her face, emphasizing her cheekbones, her delicate jawline.

But Pierce didn't remember her that way, in her gown, seated by his desk. He remembered her in his arms, underneath him, her face flushed, her eyes languorous. Her hips moving sensuously against his....

"Mr. Stanton?"

He started.

Anne was standing at the door, holding out a paper plate with a piece of chocolate cake. "It's Chelley's birthday today, so we're having a small celebration in the employee lounge. Would you like a piece of cake?"

He was silent. Hoping she hadn't seen the picture before he turned it face down on the desk top.

"If you'd like to join us, you'd be perfectly welcome."

The words were out of his mouth before he had a chance to think about them. "I can't. I've got a plane to catch."

"Mr. Stanton?" She looked confused.

"I'll be in New York over the weekend. I'm taking the rest of the day off, but I'll be back on Monday." He got up from behind his desk and reached for his coat, wool muffler and briefcase. "Thank you for the cake, Anne." Taking the paper plate out of the stunned secretary's hand, he smiled at her and started down the hall.

Admit it. You have to see her again. He'd been thinking of Valerie since she left, not wanting to admit her absence was the void in his life. Pierce had learned at a very early age it wasn't wise to need anyone;

consequently he fought his feelings all his life. What had happened with Valerie had started to crack through the careful mask he kept on his emotions.

He felt lighter, happier than he had in years. Smiling at the guard, he presented him with the piece of cake and went outside into the afternoon sunshine, dazzling against the snow.

With any luck, he'd be in New York late tonight. He had her address. He'd simply camp out on her doorstep until she had time to see him.

The something more he needed in his life was Valerie.

"YOU'RE SERIOUS?" Genie squeaked into her phone.

"They liked your performance in that Off-Broadway play a few months ago. I told you something good would come of it!" Her agent sounded triumphant, and Genie could picture Evelyn on the other end of the phone, her Bandolino shoes kicked off, reaching for a jelly bean out of the canister on her desk.

"When do they want to see me?"

"Is today too soon?"

"What time?" Genie glanced hurriedly at the clock in the kitchen.

"Be at the studio at four. Be prepared for a cold reading, but they may just go with an interview."

"Thank you, Evelyn. I'll be there."

Genie arrived at three-thirty, having treated herself to a cab. There was nothing like the prospect of a terrific audition to raise the dead. She'd been moping around the apartment that Friday morning but had called Evelyn at nine sharp. As soon as she hung up the phone, she headed for the shower.

A possible part on a brand-new soap, ''Malibu's Children,'' was nothing to sneeze at.

She felt confident about her looks. Earlier in the week, she'd had her hair professionally cut, and now it waved becomingly around her face, emphasizing her high cheekbones and her small straight nose. Wispy bangs softened her forehead. Genie loved the new freedom her hairstyle afforded her.

Her attitude going into this audition surprised her. She really didn't care whether she got it or not. Not too long ago an audition for a soap would have strung her out, made her so nervous she would have barely been able to function. But too much had happened to her. Genie had no intention of giving up her dreams—she simply had more than her ambitions on her mind.

When she walked into the office that afternoon, she quickly took note of the four people seated on one side of the rectangular table. They seemed harmless enough. She kept firmly in place the energetic smile she'd flashed when she walked in the door.

''The part we have in mind for you,'' said one of the men as he pushed a few pages of script across the table to her, ''is that of a younger seductive woman.''

She hoped her smile didn't falter, her lips wouldn't tremble.

''You're involved with a married man, an important man in the colony. You know his wife and children, but you're in love with him and you don't want him to leave you.''

She nodded her head, letting them know she understood.

One of the men seated at the table turned out to be the actor picked to play the married man. Genie looked at him and smiled, trying to make a fleeting connection with him. He didn't seem the prima donna sort.

"Take your time looking over the lines." The only woman at the table looked about forty, with stylishly cut short auburn hair and a pair of tinted glasses. Her fingernails were perfectly manicured and her makeup was flawless. Genie could feel her careful scrutiny.

She glanced down at her lines, her memory clicking them quickly into place. Words, meaningless words, unless there was emotion underlying them. She had to convince him, her lover, not to leave her. Genie studied the lines for a few more seconds, making sure she understood the intent of the scene, then looked up at the older actor and nodded almost imperceptibly.

"Joanna, it's over. I can't put Margaret through any more of this." The actor's voice was deep and resonant, classically trained.

"No." Genie looked him straight in the eye. "What I feel for you—Jared, how can you deny what we have? What we feel for each other? I don't care if you're married or what's happened to us before. I only know I love you and want to be with you the rest of my life."

And suddenly she was no longer the fictional Joanna, but Genie pleading with Pierce not to leave her. She remembered the way he had looked at her that morning in the doorway of her suite, and quick tears filled her eyes. She kept herself from crying throughout the rest of the monologue, knowing that in this case emotion held at bay would be much more powerful. Her instincts told her most actresses would play the part as a full-blown bitch, making the role a caricature. Genie played it from her gut, imbuing

Joanna with a rich interior life, with pain and passion. Human feelings.

When she finished, she looked down at the pages in her hand for just an instant to compose herself, then back at the panel. The two men were silent, but the woman was smiling and writing something on the pad in front of her.

"Do you have a picture and résumé?" she asked.

Though her agent had sent one ahead, Genie knew casting directors often asked for additional pictures. She pulled one out of her flat leather bag and handed it to her.

She was too excited to hope.

"Thank you very much." The woman looked up and offered Genie her hand.

They all shook hands; then Genie collected her things and walked quickly out of the office.

"HOW DID I DO? How the hell should I know? I was too scared." Genie tucked her scarf more tightly around her neck as she talked loudly into the pay phone, trying to make herself heard above traffic. She covered her ear with a mittened hand as a truck rumbled by. "I can't hear you, Al."

"I said I'm taking you out to dinner Saturday." Before she could reply, he continued, "I'm damn proud of you, Genie. I know you've been hurting, but you didn't let your life get in the way of this audition. You came through. Besides, we haven't toasted Kathryn Anne Jameson's birth yet."

So like Al, to think of all the aspects of her life. Early Monday morning, after only eight hours of labor, Valerie had given birth to a baby girl. Though she was still angry with her sister, Genie had swallowed her feelings and managed to concentrate on the birth. She'd been at the maternity ward that same morning with an enormous bunch of pink roses and baby's breath for Val. Studying her delicate niece through the glass, she felt the queerest mixture of sensations. Happiness for her sister. Depression at the direction in which her life seemed to be headed.

And she thought of Pierce.

"Genie? Are you there?"

"Yes. Thanks, Al. You're on."

SATURDAY MORNING, Pierce stood on the corner facing Valerie's apartment.

He didn't want to hurt her. What if her husband was home? He'd called her, but when a man had answered, he'd simply hung up.

You're behaving like a fool. But as he was chiding himself, he saw an older man, in his fifties, walk out the door and up the street, an apricot poodle on the end of a leash.

Harold. He had to be Harold. Pierce recognized him from earlier photographs. Since he'd married Valerie, both of them had become semirecluses. He was shorter than Pierce had expected, and slightly chubby. Yet he had a spring to his step, and as Pierce watched him, he called out to another man on the street. When the two met, Harold began to talk to him, his face animated.

Before he could change his mind, Pierce walked up to the doorman. Though he didn't like celebrities who used their clout to manipulate others, he did exactly that. Within minutes he was inside the elevator, on his way to the twenty-eighth floor.

Once in the elegant hallway, he hurried to the correct door. Knocking briskly, he stepped aside.

The woman who answered the door was dressed in gray sweatpants and a sweatshirt that said: Don't Bother Me, I Can't Cope. Her long dark hair was pulled back into a bun, and two pencils were stuck in her hair. Her glasses had slipped down her nose, and now she punched them back into place with her index finger.

"Harold, I knew you'd forget—" She stopped talking, simply stared at him as if seeing a ghost.

"Is Valerie home?" This had to be her mother.

"Pierce Stanton?" The woman's voice was high-pitched and nervous.

"Yes." He held out his hand. "How do you do."

She took his hand, though her grip was weak, and she didn't give her name. "I'm her sister."

"Is Valerie home?"

"Did something go wrong with the interview?" she asked, taking her glasses off and dangling them in one hand.

"No. No, this has nothing to do with the television show. I just wanted to speak to her for a moment." When the woman didn't answer, Pierce added quietly, "It's personal."

He thought he detected alarm in her eyes; then she glanced down at the carpet as if gathering her thoughts. When she met his gaze, her voice was calm.

"I'm afraid that's impossible. You see, my sister left for Europe almost a week ago. She's going to be gone for several months, researching her next book."

He felt as if she'd just given him a punch in the stomach. "Is there any way I can reach her?"

She smiled but stood firmly in the doorway, and it

seemed to Pierce she was trying to block his view into the penthouse. "I'm afraid not. You see, my sister is ruled by her impulses. She travels from city to city and phones us every few weeks. We have to rely on her calls because we never know where she'll be from day to day. But," she added, "I'll be sure to tell her you came by. Is there a number where you can be reached?"

He dug into his coat pocket and extracted a business card. "I'll be in Chicago only a few more weeks. I'm moving to New York."

She took the card, studied it. "All right, Mr. Stanton. And please notify the front desk before you come next time." Without another word, she stepped back and shut the door quietly.

Chapter Eight

Back inside his hotel room, Pierce lay down on the bed and stared at the ceiling.

Why had she left so suddenly? How would he ever find her? Would she call him when she found out he'd been to her apartment, or would she be angry with him? He'd taken a risk going to see her.

But she was gone. At the moment, that was all that mattered. He had built this moment up in his mind, had anticipated seeing her....

A married woman. He tried to stop the images that flashed through his mind one after another. Images of Valerie, the way she looked up into his face, her laughter, her expression as she unbuttoned her gown and let it fall to the floor of her suite...

With a groan, Pierce stood up and grabbed his keys. He had to get out, walk, do anything but sit in his hotel room and think about Valerie.

Later that evening, having eaten a light dinner and walked several blocks in the cold November air, Pierce came back to his hotel room and prepared for bed.

Lying on his back, staring unseeing at the television set, he finally admitted what hurt the most.

You're a coward. He reached for the light next to

his bed and turned it off. *You're a coward. You should have stayed with her after that night. Something could have been worked out. You don't take feelings like you have for Valerie lightly. But you were afraid.*

He sighed deeply, then flung his arm over his eyes, blocking out the flickering image of the screen. Though he lay perfectly still, his mind worked feverishly.

There had to be a way to find her. To let her know how much he cared.

"COME ON, Genie, eat up! It's not every week you audition for a soap!" Al poured her another glass of wine, then handed her a piece of garlic bread.

Genie knew she ought to feel on top of the world, but she couldn't pretend anymore. The wine tasted flat, the eggplant lasagna felt like lead in her stomach, and the garlic bread threatened a return journey. It was too hot and crowded in the restaurant. She wanted to go home.

"Al?"

"Are you okay, Genie?"

She shook her head. "Can we just go back to your place? I don't think I'm up to dessert."

They walked back to his apartment, where he made two cups of herbal tea and carried them out to the sofa. His gray tabby cat, Oscar, was curled up on Genie's feet.

"Drink this." He set the tea down in front of her, on a coffee table made of bricks and boards.

She took a sip, then set it down.

"Genie, if you don't call this man, I'm going to call him for you. I've never seen anyone act so disgustingly noble in my entire life."

She traced her finger lightly over the nubby material of the sofa. She and Al had picked it up off the street. Both their apartments had been furnished mostly with castoffs, then livened up with green plants, a coat of paint and the granny-square afghans she crocheted in her spare time. She thought again of how lucky she was to have him as a friend.

"You're losing weight, Al. You look a lot better." She wanted to change the subject. Al had already been subjected to too many analytic phone calls late at night. Always about Pierce. She'd thought she would stop thinking about him once she returned to New York. But she'd been wrong about that, too.

"Thanks." Al reached over and lightly covered her hand with his. "Don't evade the issue. This is me, remember? Call him, Genie, please. If he's the type of guy you think he is, he'll understand."

The wall in front of her eyes began to blur, all the books on the shelves blending together in a riot of colors. Slowly Genie covered her eyes with her hands, pulled her legs up underneath her body. She felt Al's arms come around her comfortingly.

"I can't stand it anymore," she whispered. "I never knew it could hurt like this, not being with someone." Tired of holding her emotions tightly in check, Genie began to cry.

"Oh, Genie." Al simply held her, stroked her hair, let her take strength from him. When she finished crying, using up almost an entire box of tissues, he went back into the kitchen and put another pot of water to boil.

He came back into the small living room with a plate of her favorite cookies from a nearby Italian bakery. Buttery cookies, dipped in semisweet chocolate.

Though she started to protest, he pushed her objections aside. "There's nothing like chocolate for a broken heart. Eat these. I'm going to get your beeper out of your purse, check your messages, give you a shoulder massage, walk you home and tuck you in. No arguments."

She nodded her head. It felt strange, having someone else take care of her, but her sleepless nights were beginning to catch up with her.

When Al came back, she was almost asleep. She felt him tuck the afghan around her, then heard him pick up the cookie plate and empty teacups before she fell asleep.

SHE WANTED to call Pierce during the next few days, but she hesitated. It seemed an impersonal way to explain her deception, over the phone. And being in limbo was better than facing his contempt—at least there was still a small modicum of hope in simply drifting.

She spent Thanksgiving with her mother, in the house she'd grown up in. Valerie and Harold had suddenly made other plans, and Genie decided a quiet retreat to her mother's wouldn't be a bad holiday.

She lost herself in the familiar holiday rituals. Genie loved her mother's kitchen, all warm wood and copper pots. Valerie had bought the house for their mother when she married Harold. Genie remembered her older sister's disgust when Madame Bouchet had later refused to leave the house; Valerie had wanted to buy something much larger for her, but Madame had stood firm. So Val remodeled the little house, and now the kitchen sported a stone fireplace, a small greenhouse for fresh vegetables and a skylight. Yet Genie had to smile—Val had so little understanding of their mother. Though Madame had the latest electric juicer known to mankind, she still sliced and juiced her oranges by hand every morning. Old habits were hard to break.

Genie was home again, with reassuring sights and smells surrounding her. She basked in the warmth of her mother's company, thankful for a respite from life.

Dinner was a lively affair. Having lost her husband shortly after Genie was born, Madame knew about loneliness. Thus she made it a practice to invite to her home people who were alone in the world. Thanksgivings and Christmases had never been dull—a soldier here, an exchange student there. Many of the old people in the neighborhood were regulars, and all enjoyed Madame's warmth and sincere hospitality.

The morning after Thanksgiving Day Genie and her mother were alone for breakfast.

"Come sit with me," Madame said, putting two cups of black coffee on a tray and carrying it out to the large sunny family room in the back of the house. Madame was still slim and quick, and her long hair was lustrous, though lightly sprinkled with gray.

They sat on opposite ends of the couch. Plants ran riot everywhere, attesting to Madame Bouchet's love of indoor gardening.

Genie fixed her mother's coffee, then her own. Though she'd still been depressed when she left Manhattan, she felt she'd done an excellent job of hiding her feelings from her mother. But Genie didn't want to worry her. Her mother had gone through enough with Valerie.

She could feel her mother's gaze on her. "Do you want a piece of this apple tart?" Genie asked.

"Tell me what bothers you, Genie." Her voice was low, the slight French accent softening the sounds of the words.

"How did you know?" She hadn't had to say a single word. It had always been that way, even when she was a child. Valerie had told anyone within hearing distance how she was feeling; Genie always contained her emotions.

"Because I try to see with the heart, not the eye. Tell me. Whatever bothers you, it will help to share it."

Genie remained silent, staring at the coffee cup she held in her hand.

"A man?" Her mother's voice was encouraging.

Genie set her coffee down. "You always guess."

Madame Bouchet smiled, a funny little smile that barely moved her expressive mouth. "You carry yourself so tightly, as if holding in enough pain for the entire family. Your eyes are tired, and you don't smile and laugh as you usually do."

"I'm glad I came home."

Her mother set down her coffee, then turned on the couch so she faced Genie and took both her hands in her own. "Tell me, and we can share your pain together. It never helps to carry it alone. I know a little bit about love. Perhaps I can help you."

Genie hesitated, then blurted out, "You would never have gotten yourself in such a mess in the first place!"

Madame laughed quietly. "That is because you see me as your mother, not as a woman."

Slowly, haltingly, Genie told her mother the entire story, starting with Valerie's request and ending with her lonely flight back to New York. But she left out the night Pierce spent in her suite.

Madame studied her daughter's face closely. "This man, did he try to make love to you?" She asked the question as delicately as possible.

Genie felt her face flame, and tears welled up in her eyes. "No. He was...the perfect gentleman. I was the one. I trapped him in my room Friday night, and—"

"And you behaved as two people in love have behaved throughout the centuries. I've lived long enough, my darling, that not much surprises me. And so you love this man?"

Genie nodded, miserable.

"You must tell him your feelings."

She looked at her mother, shocked.

"Oh, Genie! Don't look at me that way! I know you think I am wrong, but if you listen, you will agree. From what you have told me, he sounds like an honorable man, this Pierce. He fought for his sister, he stood for his beliefs. He is a man who will love as strongly as he hates, who will do anything for the woman he loves."

"Then why did he leave me?" Genie asked.

"Was he trying to be strong for you? He had nothing to lose by loving you. But you did. A husband."

Genie stared down at her hands. She could still remember the tight expression on Pierce's face the morning he left her suite. What her mother was saying made sense—a selfish man *would* have stayed. And Pierce had left.

"You must tell him you are free to love him."

"But the interview!"

"Valerie is—Valerie is my daughter, but she is also one who thinks only of herself. She should have never sent you to do that interview. She could have rescheduled it after Kathryn was born, or she could have refused, as she has done before. She was thinking, as always, only of Valerie. You must never let family feelings sway you toward something you do not want to do.''

Genie nodded slowly. She had followed Valerie around all her life, looking up to her older sister with a sense of hero worship. But she had to begin seeing her sister as the person she was. And she had to stop jumping at her beck and call.

''Also, this man—Genie, one of the hardest parts of loving is that you are no longer alone.''

''I thought that would be the easiest part,'' Genie said.

''No, that is the popular thought. It is very hard to love someone because you are no longer just yourself. You have to—how do you say—get inside someone's skin and see the world as he sees it. Can you see Pierce this way?''

Genie closed her eyes.

Madame's gentle voice continued. ''I see him as a man who is very lonely. Where is his family? He lives all alone in that house by the lake with his dogs, but except for his sister, he mentions no one else in his life. He works very hard on his show, but perhaps it is to take the place of what he doesn't have. Then you come into his life, a woman he would never have met. He is confused, because he desires you and despises you at the same time. But the longer he knows you, the more he loves you.''

Genie could feel the tears behind her eyes, and she tried to hold them back.

''A man can make love to many women,'' her

mother said quietly. "But there are only one or two times in a lifetime—if he's lucky—when he experiences..." She paused, and Genie knew she was searching for the right word. "Experiences a love so strong it almost lifts him out of his body. *That* is love, that is worth fighting for. That is what I believe he feels for you."

"Then why doesn't he call me?"

"Why would he call you? He would call Valerie. But he would hesitate to call her, for hurting her. Or hurting Harold. This Pierce, he is a dangerous combination. He loves passionately, and he is an honorable man."

"So I need to call him."

"You see? And it will not be hard, because he will be so happy to hear from you."

GENIE TRIED to reach Pierce at the studio, but the switchboard operator told her they were closed for the holidays.

She thought about him for the rest of the holiday, pictured him at his house, alone with Jaime and Parrish. Did some friends invite him to their home so he wouldn't spend Thanksgiving alone? Did he think of her at all, as she was thinking of him?

The next morning she said goodbye to her mother and took the train to the city. As the bare trees and snow-covered buildings flashed by, Genie was already beginning to count the hours until she talked to Pierce.

But the first person she talked to on Monday was her agent.

"Good morning, Joanna."

"Joanna—Joanna, as in 'Malibu's Children'?"

"They want you at the studio as soon as possible for costume fittings. Congratulations, Genie."

Al came over that night and fixed dinner. He opened a bottle of champagne with a flourish, then made a toast.

"Here's hoping you become the biggest bitch on afternoon television!" He grinned boyishly as he handed her a glass.

"Thanks, Al. God, what would I do without you?"

"I don't even want to contemplate that sort of existence." He took a sip of champagne and set the glass down on the kitchen table. "Did you call him?"

"Pierce?"

"No, the tooth fairy. Of course, Pierce!"

"I—I had to go straight down for costume fittings. I thought I'd have time to slip away, but—"

"Tomorrow?" he said sternly.

"Tomorrow." She nodded, and they touched glasses.

"I'D LIKE to speak with Pierce Stanton, please." Genie stood out in the hall of the studio in a glittery slinky creation.

"Who shall I say is calling?"

"Tell him it's—Valerie."

She was put on hold. Genie glanced nervously at the clock. She was due back on the set in twenty minutes. Closing her eyes, she willed Pierce to come to the phone.

The receptionist clicked back on. "He's in conference right now and cannot be disturbed. Shall I give him a message?"

Genie thought wildly. She couldn't give him Val's number and she didn't know when she'd be home. If he called her number, he'd get her machine. She didn't want to confuse him.

"I'll call back." She hung up.

She called again the next day and got Anne on the phone.

"He didn't renew his contract."

"He what!" Genie said. "When?"

"He told me he was leaving after he came back from New York—"

"When did he go to New York?"

"Right after Thanksgiving. He was back the following week, and that's when he told us he wasn't signing on again."

"But what's he going to do?"

Anne sighed. "He said something about finding out exactly what he wanted."

Genie blinked back sudden tears. "Good for him."

"Do you want me to tell him you called? He's in a meeting."

"No." She didn't want Pierce to try to reach Valerie. Genie didn't want her to know she was going to reveal the entire masquerade. "What's the best time to reach him?"

"I'd try early in the morning. The rest of the day he's busy."

"Okay. Thanks, Anne."

"Oh, and Valerie? My mother loved the books you sent her."

THE NEXT WEEK proved to be full for Genie. She was required on the set every single day. During the few minutes she had to herself she didn't dare leave. She fell into a working routine: up early in the morning, at the studio by seven, home by nine. A quick supper, then straight to bed.

She thought about Pierce during the moments before she fell asleep. She'd visualize his smile, his intense gaze, the way he'd looked at her after the first time they made love. Then she would drift off to sleep, promising herself she would call him tomorrow.

Deep inside she knew: she was scared. If Pierce had despised Valerie for deceiving his sister, how would he feel about her deception? Would he ever be able to trust her again? Would he even want a relationship with her? What had they had, after all? One night. It wasn't a lot to build a relationship on.

But her instincts won out. There was something very special between them, and she had to risk everything to find out if it was still there. Genie made her decision on the way to work one morning. She'd fly to Chicago when taping finished, before Christmas. She wanted to be with Pierce when she told him, wanted to see his face when she explained why she'd impersonated her sister.

It was not something she wanted to tell him over the phone.

PIERCE PLACED the last of his books on the shelves, then stepped back and surveyed the results. He liked it. He headed back toward the kitchen of his new apartment and opened the refrigerator, taking out a small carton of orange juice. The last few days had left him exhausted, but it had been worth it.

He'd accomplished the impossible. He'd found the strength to leave a job that hadn't satisfied him for almost a year. He'd found an apartment near Valerie's. He'd rented out his house to a young married couple who were willing to take care of Jaime and Parrish for a year.

That gave him one year to win Valerie.

In the evenings, he took walks by her building, occasionally catching glimpses of Harold and his poodle.

And Valerie was still in Europe.

He took a long swallow of juice and set the carton down on the kitchen table. His apartment was shaping up better than he'd imagined. He'd already made the master bedroom habitable, while the other bedroom was still full of boxes. He'd had some of the furniture shipped from his house in Evanston, just enough to give the apartment a familiar feeling.

He glanced at his watch when he heard a brisk knock on the door. Barbara was right on schedule. One of the added bonuses of moving to New York was that he'd be able to see his older sister more often.

Pierce opened the door, enveloping in a quick hug the tall, dark-haired woman who stood there. "You must be freezing. Get in here."

Time had changed Barbara a great deal. The evening she'd come to his house after her husband's betrayal, she'd been completely destroyed. The classic dependent housewife, she had no idea what to do with her life. She only knew she had to get away from her husband.

Pierce had helped her as much as possible. When she finally decided to try screen and television writing, he encouraged her to go back to school. After her graduation, he called their father and made him use every connection at his disposal. And Barbara had worked her way up from secretary to the head writer of the soap "Promise of Tomorrow."

"I'm sorry I'm late," she began.

"Barb, you're right on time."

"I mean, I'm sorry I had to agree to see you so late in the day." She took a moment to look around the apartment. "I can't believe you moved in here two days ago! It looks practically finished!"

He grinned. "Just don't look in the back bedroom."

They spent the rest of the evening talking. Pierce tactfully avoided the real reason he was in New York, not wanting to cause Barbara any remembered pain. He'd tell her in time. She regaled him with a number of anecdotes about the people she worked with.

"And you can't *believe* what's going to happen with Jonathan." She laughed and fell back among the sofa cushions. "Pierce, I've worked out all my feelings about Robert by making terrible things happen to Jonathan."

After the laughter subsided, she grew serious. "But you can't just stay locked up in this apartment. Why don't you come down to my office tomorrow and I'll take you out to lunch?"

"I've got nothing else to do," he teased.

"You brat!"

"What time do you take lunch?" Pierce asked as he walked her outside and hailed a taxi.

"When you arrive. See you tomorrow."

GENIE COULD HARDLY contain her apprehension. Her flight to Chicago hadn't given her enough time to prepare what she was going to say to Pierce. She had decided to take him out to lunch and tell him the entire story, from the beginning.

She poked her head cautiously into his office, then smiled as she saw Anne, busy at her word processor.

"Hi, stranger."

"Valerie! What are *you* doing here?"

"Just checking on old friends. Where's Pierce?" Genie congratulated herself on achieving just the right amount of nonchalance.

"Pierce?" Anne's face fell, and for a second Genie panicked. What had happened to him?

"Pierce left last week. I thought I told you he was leaving us."

Genie sat down on the leather couch and pulled off her gloves, then her scarf. "You told me. But how did he leave so quickly? I thought he had all sorts of things to sort out?"

"He did." Anne grimaced. "I have to admit, as much as I like Pierce, he was pretty hard to work with near the end. I swear, he acted as if he was possessed."

"Where is he now?" Genie asked quietly.

"I guess he's at home in Evanston. I can give you his phone number if you'd like it. Just don't let anyone know how you got it."

"Anne." Genie moistened her lips. "Could you do me one last favor?"

"Sure."

"Could you just give me his address? What I have to talk to him about needs to be said in person."

"I have it right here. Just a sec."

As Genie copied it down, along with instructions on how to get to Evanston, she felt her anxiety blossoming all over again. But she was excited, too.

Within an hour she'd see him.

WITHIN AN HOUR Genie was certain she had been crazy to fly out to Chicago.

The house looked exactly as she'd seen it last. Except Pierce wasn't there.

"He said he was going to New York for a year," said Cindy, a young blonde with vivid blue eyes.

Her husband, Alan, shot her a warning glance. "Honey, I'm not sure Mr. Stanton would want us telling his plans to everyone."

"But darling, I *know* Valerie. I've read every single one of her books!"

After several autographs and a promise to stop by if she was ever in town again, Genie drove back to the airport.

As she flew back, all she could think of was that Pierce was in New York. And he had to be looking for her.

Chapter Nine

Pierce walked wearily out of a small corner grocery. How could essentially doing nothing be harder work than what he had done at the studio? Yet he was finding this to be true. Deciding he needed to get some exercise, he'd jogged down the street and done his weekly shopping. He had enough food in the shopping bag in his arms to last another week.

But if he was honest with himself, it was more than simply doing nothing. He missed Valerie. And he couldn't seem to find her, no matter how he tried. It was as if she'd vanished into thin air. Though he watched the front of her apartment building every night and made discreet inquiries, he had no luck. Now it was almost Christmas, and still no sign of her. The thought was depressing.

It was getting too cold to walk the rest of the six blocks back, so he decided to take a bus. Once inside the slow-moving vehicle, he balanced the heavy grocery bag on his hip and held on to the overhead pole.

He watched the crowds of people on the sidewalks as the bus lumbered by. The shop windows were decorated with twinkling lights and greenery, all signs of Christmas. The snow on the sidewalk was tightly packed, but flakes were beginning to drift down softly out of the deep-gray sky.

Then he saw her.

She was dressed in a bright-red heavy sweater, a pair of jeans, colorful embroidered mittens and a matching hat. Valerie was jogging in the opposite direction, a small black dog trotting along on a leash beside her.

Pierce lunged for the bell, pulling the thin wire as if trying to break it. But the bus had just passed its designated stop, so it kept moving, up the next block.

He struggled to the front of the bus, past work-weary people, mothers with small children, and a few bums.

"I have to get off!"

"Next stop," the driver intoned automatically, not looking at him.

Once the bus stopped, Pierce pushed through the press of bodies crowding to get on, then set off in the direction he'd seen her.

Valerie! The thought of seeing her again made his feet fly over the packed snow. People turned as he ran past them, his bag of groceries clutched tightly against his chest.

But by the time he reached the spot where he'd seen her, she was gone. He kept running for a while, searching in vain for a glimpse of her bright-red sweater, her long black hair.

But she had disappeared.

HE CALLED her sister from the downstairs desk in her apartment building that night, his voice clogged and nasal from the cold air.

"This is Pierce Stanton. Is Valerie home?"

"No. No, she's not. I thought I told you she was in Europe, doing research for her next—"

"I *know* what you told me, but I saw her today. Does she have a little black dog?"

"No, she doesn't. You must have seen someone else, Mr. Stanton."

He sighed, his expression one of pure frustration. "Look, I don't mean any harm to your sister. Please, when you speak to her, will you remember to tell her Pierce Stanton has been trying to reach her?"

"I will, Mr. Stanton. Good night."

He stared at the dead phone for a second, then slammed it into its cradle.

IN THE END, when they met again it was so simple that Genie wondered if they had been fated to be together no matter what happened.

She was coming home from some last-minute Christmas shopping when she decided to get off the subway by Valerie's apartment and stop at her favorite florist's. Genie had been angry with her sister, so she decided to buy her two pots of white poinsettias as a peace offering. The display of flowers was outside the shop in a heated glass enclosure on the sidewalk, and as she bent down and picked up one of the plants, she heard his voice.

"Valerie!"

She turned, almost dropping the pot. He was running down the block toward her.

She didn't stop to think. All her carefully prepared speeches flew out of her head when she saw him. She took one step out of the shop, then two more; then she was swept up in his passionate embrace, into his arms. His lips came down over hers in a kiss so full of longing it took her breath away. They continued to kiss as she slid slowly down his body, her arms wrapped tightly around his neck.

When they broke apart, they continued to stare at each other, as if each couldn't believe the other was really there.

"Pierce, how did you—"

He spoke at the same moment. "When did you get home—"

"Lady, do you want these poinsettias or not? I gotta close up and get home." The florist was trying to look stern but not succeeding.

"She wants them." Pierce reached quickly into his coat pocket and took out his wallet. After paying the man, he hoisted both pots into his arms. "Let's go."

"Where are we going?" she asked breathlessly.

"Back to my apartment."

"You live here?" She was incredulous.

He grinned. "Carry one of these pots so I can put my arm around you."

With both hands holding the foil-wrapped pot, Genie felt the warmth of his embrace as his arm came around her; then he caught her closely against his side.

"Do you mind?" he asked, leaning over to give her a quick kiss.

"No." Genie felt as if she'd been sleepwalking before this moment. How had she lived without him in her life? Then she remembered. She had to tell him before they reached his apartment—and his bed.

"Pierce, there's something I have to tell you—"

"No." His voice was firm, with a hint of strain behind it. "I've been looking for you for too long. I want the next few hours for us. Anything that needs to be said can wait a little longer."

"YOU HAVE NO IDEA how much I missed you," Pierce said as he came back into his bedroom with a bottle of champagne and two glasses. "I almost went out of my mind waiting for you to come back into my life."

Genie lay back against the pillows, feeling cherished and complete. "I missed you, too."

They toasted each other silently with their eyes. She couldn't look at him enough, couldn't fill her senses with the reality that he was here. And he still cared for her.

Pierce set down his glass on the table by the bed, then reached for her hand. "I still don't feel that I've welcomed you back into my life properly."

Genie laughed, feeling light and warm from their first frenzied lovemaking. "And what could you possibly do to make me feel more welcome than I do now?"

He reached for her glass and set it down next to his. "Oh, I think I have a few tricks up my sleeve. But you have to help me."

She looked up at him, feigning innocence, as he moved over her. "What do you want me to do?"

He threaded his fingers through her hair, tilted her face closer to his. "I want to hear you say it," he murmured huskily, kissing the curve of her neck. "I want you to say 'Kiss me.'"

She smiled. Waiting. Teasing.

He frowned with mock impatience. "Say 'Kiss me.'" He leaned over and bit her gently on the neck.

"Kiss me," she whispered.

He did, slowly parting his lips, exploring her with exquisite delight, taking his time. She was warm and fluid and open underneath him, pulling him closer, wanting to feel every part of his body, wanting to recapture the passion they'd shared moments before.

He was only kissing her, but she felt as if she were burning with fever, being consumed amid waves of undulating heat. She ran her fingers over his shoulders, eased his head closer to hers, increased the pressure of the kiss. She wanted him, wanted to feel him inside her, wanted to reach pure pleasure.

He broke the kiss, then traced the line of her lips with his finger, touching the corner of her mouth gently.

"Now say 'I want you,'" he whispered.

"I want you." Her mouth trembled as she softly voiced her desire.

"Again. Say it again."

"I want you. So much." Her voice was barely a whisper.

They didn't say anything more for a long time.

"VALERIE?"

"Shhh. Go back to sleep."

"Where are you going?"

"I have to go home."

Pierce sat up and reached for his pants. "I'll take you. I won't have you out alone at this hour."

She stopped dressing. If he saw her to her apartment, he would know she wasn't Valerie. No best-selling author lived in the neighborhood she did.

But didn't she want him to know? Hadn't that been the point of seeing him again, to tell him the truth? It had been so easy, felt so right to be back in his arms, making love for hours. Why couldn't she feel comfortable about telling him the truth?

I'll tell him tomorrow, she thought quickly, not

wanting to admit she was lying to herself. She couldn't go home now.

She started to take off her clothes.

"What are you doing?" His voice was concerned.

"I've decided to stay."

His face relaxed. "I wanted to wake up and find you here with me."

She felt her throat tighten. "Oh, Pierce." And then she was back in his arms.

But afterward, lying next to him in bed, Genie had to admit to herself she was a coward.

What? Are you afraid he won't love you when you tell him you impersonated your sister?

He has such impossibly high standards, she answered herself.

If he really loves you, he'll understand.

But I did it mostly...for the money. And I wonder if he could ever understand doing something for money.

His family couldn't have made all its money playing fair.

But he always has.

She turned slightly away from him on the king-sized bed.

I'll tell him tomorrow. I couldn't bear if he left again.

Chapter Ten

But she didn't tell him. The next two days blended together, an emotional kaleidoscope of enjoyment with Pierce. Showing him the parts of the city she loved. Walking in Central Park, going to an afternoon movie, exploring the Metropolitan Museum, riding the ferry to the Statue of Liberty. They had dinner in Little Italy and afterward stopped at Genie's favorite ice-cream store, a family-owned shop with the best *gelati* in New York.

And always, Pierce. Genie sensed he'd always been a serious man, even as a little boy. She wanted him to play. So she took a short holiday from her life. Shooting had stopped for the holidays, so her days were her own. They played and played and played, like two tourists from out of town.

But in the back of her mind the knowledge of her deception hung over her, and Genie knew she couldn't delay telling Pierce the truth. She'd taken these days to solidify what they had, to build another link in their relationship. To ground things.

Yet the truth still stood between them. He had to be told.

THREE NIGHTS after Pierce had found her, Genie lay awake in his arms. There wasn't such a thing as a good time to tell Pierce. The knowledge wasn't going to be welcomed, no matter how she phrased it.

She tried out several approaches in the safety of her mind.

Oh, by the way, Pierce, I'm not really Valerie Bouchet. She's my sister.

She closed her eyes and grimaced. *Better try harder than that.*

Oh, Pierce, I know I should have told you sooner, but my name is Genie and I'm an actress. Such a good actress that my sister hired me to do her interview for her. And I was just incapable of saying no.

That certainly wasn't any better. Genie took a deep breath, then turned gently over on her back, away from Pierce. She stared at the ceiling.

What can I tell you that will make you feel better about what I did? That I was tired of standing on my feet all day, taking orders from people, cleaning up after they ate? That I wanted a chance to be something more than a waitress? That I've been at Val's beck and call since I was three years old and it's been a damn hard habit to break?

She sighed again, no closer to an answer.

That I did it for Val, and the money. The freedom. Can you ever understand that?

She watched him as he slept, wishing she had the courage to wake him up and tell him everything. As she studied his face, she made a promise to herself. She wouldn't go on deceiving the man she loved.

You gave yourself two or three days with him, no more. You cannot go on without telling him. Even if it means losing him.

Voicing her deepest fears made it hurt less. Snuggling back down underneath the covers, she finally relaxed. At last—a definite deadline in her mind. A turning point in their relationship.

Pierce would understand.

GENIE HELD the phone receiver between her shoulder and her ear as she sliced the slightly frozen sirloin into thin strips. "Why should I worry? It's only a party." She could hear Al's sigh over the phone.

"Nothing. I just worry." Al's voice was full of concern. "I wish you'd tell him and be done with it."

Genie paused, her knife still. "I've got it all planned out. Pierce is taking his sister, Barbara, to this party tonight. I made him promise not to eat too much because I'm making us dinner. Then tonight, when we're alone, I'm going to tell him."

Al didn't seem convinced. "Call me in the morning and let me now how it went. I'll be up late if you need me." He hesitated, and it seemed he wanted to say more but didn't.

"Everything's going to be fine," Genie said, more to assure herself than Al. "I'll call you. Maybe we can have lunch later in the week, okay?"

"YOUR NEW girl friend is a doll to let you out the door so close to Christmas," Barbara said as Pierce helped her navigate the icy street toward their waiting taxi. "You know how I hate parties, so going with you makes it bearable."

"Thanks...I think." Pierce grinned at his sister, then eased her inside the waiting vehicle. Sliding in next to her, he closed the door firmly and gave the driver their destination. Both of them loosened their coats and settled down for the drive.

After a few minutes of silence, Barbara reached for his hand and squeezed it. "There's another reason I'm glad you're with me tonight."

"What's that?"

Her fingers tightened around his. "*She's* going to be there tonight."

Pierce felt as if someone had reached inside his stomach and was tearing at his insides. *Valerie?*

"'She,' as in Valerie Bouchet?"

Barbara nodded. "I'm ready to see her again. She won't remember me. But that was part of the reason I didn't want to go without you. I need your support. It's still hard to look at her and remember—" She stopped talking abruptly and stared out at the snow-covered streets.

Pierce squeezed her hand gently, thoughts whirling through his head.

Why hadn't she told him? Was this Val's idea of a joke? Didn't she realize what seeing her again would do to Barbara? But then he remembered what she'd said as he'd walked out of the door. *I have my own plans for the evening, Pierce.* How could she have known Barbara was going to attend this particular party when he hadn't even known until just now? Valerie did have a right to a life of her own.

He was startled out of his thoughts when Barbara took his hand. "I think I'm closer to you than just about anyone," she said. "I guess that's why I wanted you with me tonight."

"Were you ever—angry with Valerie?"

Barbara shook her head, her chin-length hair brushing her cheeks gently. "No. Robert had been cheating on me long before he met her. In a perverse sort of way, she was a blessing in disguise.''

''Why?'' He had to know how his sister felt about Valerie before they reached the party.

''He was so blatant about their affair—and it made me so angry I finally decided to divorce him.'' Barbara laughed softly. ''In a way, I feel like going up to her and thanking her. I might still be in Robert's house, with dinner on the table, waiting for him to come home.''

''But that night—''

''It hurt. I loved him when I married him. But when I look back on everything, I'm glad I got out when I did.'' She glanced outside her window. ''I think this is the place.''

As the taxi pulled up in front of the hotel, Pierce stopped thinking long enough to pay the driver and help his sister out of the cab. Then, with his protective arm around her shoulder, they entered the building.

It was an old hotel, facing Central Park, and the doorman was aloof and courteous as he admitted them. Pierce remained silent during the long ascent, but as soon as they stepped out of the elevator they were assailed with laughter, cigarette smoke and the mixed scents of expensive perfumes coming from the open suite door.

Barbara reached for his arm as if it were the only steady thing in the universe at that moment, and Pierce fixed a smile on his face. *If she looks as bad as I feel, we're one hell of a couple.* He didn't want to see Valerie in public, didn't want to play out a false, polite charade for public benefit.

He'd never fully realized how strongly he felt about her.

They gave their coats to the maid at the door. Pierce patted Barbara's arm reassuringly and began to weave his way gently through the crush of people. There was so much noise he could barely think. But he knew whom he was looking for. Valerie.

And then he saw her.

She was at the far end of the room, sitting on a sofa with Harold. They were looking into each other's eyes, arms entwined, drinking champagne. Her back was to him, so all he could see was her upswept hair, the graceful length of her neck, her bare shoulders. Diamonds sparkled on her ears and spilled over her neck, the elegant necklace catching what little light was in the room. Her face was barely in profile.

"Pierce, you're hurting my arm." It was a few seconds before he realized Barbara was speaking to him. Gently he released her, then turned to face her.

"Barbara, I have some business to attend to. Can I leave you for just a minute?"

She nodded. "I'll be by the bar."

As Pierce crossed the room, he felt as if a giant hand were squeezing his heart. Was it possible to feel so much jealousy and still be standing? Across the room, the woman he had made love to for the past three days was talking—*flirting*—with another man. He didn't give a damn if Harold was her husband—Valerie couldn't feel the way she did about him and her husband as well!

He was damned if he was going to be caught in the middle.

"Hello, Valerie. It's good to see you again." He managed to thrust the words out. His feelings were raw with anger raging within him. He wanted to pull her out of Harold's arms and carry her down the stairs, back to his apartment.

"Hello, Mr.—" The words died in the air as Valerie looked up and saw who was looking down at her.

Pierce narrowed his eyes in disbelief. *This* wasn't Valerie! This was her sister, the woman who had met him at Valerie's apartment. The woman who had told him Valerie was in Europe. The woman who had answered his impassioned questions with cool indifference.

Slowly, ever so slowly, Pierce reached down, took her delicate wrist in his fingers, tightened his hold and pulled her to her feet.

"Smile, Valerie. You and I are going over to the bar to get something to drink. And then you're going to tell me exactly what the hell is going on."

PIERCE GAZED UP at the front of his apartment building, his eyes narrowing against the cold night air as he counted up the stories, found his window.

She was up there. *Geneviève. Genie.* He rolled her name around in his mouth, and it left a bitter taste.

Just how much of Geneviève's acting had gone into her role? She'd been very convincing as a guest on his show. As a best-selling author. As a passionate woman in his bed.

He shut his eyes against the sudden shaft of intense pain. He had thought she was something special. Believed their relationship had been worth taking her out of marriage.

Now everything Valerie had told him played over and over in his mind.

"She did it for the money, Mr. Stanton. Genie wants to be an actress, but she isn't having much success, so when I offered her this part, she jumped at the chance. You see, I've been ill—''

Valerie was sick, all right. The entire situation was sick.

His anger had mounted steadily throughout the evening. He'd seen Barbara home, then asked the driver to drop him off several blocks before his apartment, hoping the walk would cool him off.

It hadn't.

Get it over with. With a feeling of grim determination, he started toward his apartment. And the stranger who was waiting.

GENIE MOVED quickly around the apartment, checking to make sure everything was in readiness for Pierce's return. There were logs in the fireplace, with just enough tinder to create a cheerful fire. All the ingredients for her ginger beef stir fry were sliced and ready in the refrigerator. The apartment was dark, except for the candles she had burning on the dining-room table.

Perfect.

The sound of a key turning in the lock brought her to the door. Pierce entered slowly, his face averted from hers.

''Did you have a good time with Barbara?''

''It was interesting.''

She watched him as he took off his coat, his muffler, his overshoes. His dark hair had been ruffled by the wind, and he smoothed it back with an impatient gesture.

''Are you ready for dinner?'' she asked brightly. He seemed a little distant. Perhaps he was tired. He didn't seem to be the same man who had left her earlier.

''Fine.''

She frowned, then decided she was overreacting because she was nervous. Though she was sure this was the right time to tell Pierce, it still wasn't going to be easy.

"I'll get things started, then." She turned away from him and started to walk into the kitchen.

"You do that, Geneviève."

It took a moment for her name to register. When it did, she felt her heart start to pound, sending blood through her veins with dizzying speed. Slowly she turned, looked up into his eyes.

The betrayed expression on his face was far more eloquent than anything he could have said. Candlelight softened the sharp planes of his face, but his eyes were guarded. Waiting.

Tears blurred her vision. She'd longed for the day he would use her name but never dreamed that when he finally did, his voice would be filled with such contempt.

"Pierce, I was going to tell you—"

He held up his hand, silencing her. And Genie wished he would yell or scream. Anything was preferable to this tightly controlled stranger.

"I'm sure you were. After you finished your little game, I'm sure I was meant to know everything. But how much did Valerie pay you for that?" As he spoke, he gestured in the direction of his bedroom.

"No!" The word burst out of her mouth, a sound of pure pain. "You're wrong! I—"

"Please. I don't want to hear it."

After the most uncomfortable moment of silence she'd ever endured, Genie nervously wet her lips and asked quietly, "How did you find out?"

He sighed deeply, then walked away from her until

he stood in front of the living-room window, looking out into the evening sky. "Valerie was at the party. We had a nice little talk."

There was nothing she could say.

He laughed, a short bitter sound. "Did the two of you have a good laugh the day I came by her apartment?"

"You *what!*"

"I looked all over town for you. The first place I stopped was at Valerie's. She told me you were in Europe."

"Oh, God," she replied quietly.

They were quiet for a moment longer. The sight of Pierce's stiff back was Genie's emotional undoing. She had to reach him.

"Pierce, please believe me. I was going to tell—"

He turned toward her with an anger so intense she backed away. "*When?* I laid my *soul* out to you, I *trusted* you, and you deceived me! What the hell was going on in your head? Or was it all some big joke between you and that—your sister."

"I was going to tell you." Genie started toward him, but the look in his eyes made her stop.

"When? When I came out here looking for you? When I left my job in Chicago? When I met you on the street and we came back upstairs and went straight to bed?" She couldn't be sure, but it seemed his eyes were unnaturally bright. *"When were you planning on telling me who in the hell you are?"*

She hung her head, her throat thick with unshed tears. There was no way out of this nightmare. Her own actions cast her in the worst light possible.

"Tonight. I was going to tell you tonight."

"Tonight." His voice was heavily sarcastic.

Some of her fighting spirit came back. *Make him understand.* She looked up at him, pushing her hair out of her eyes with an angry gesture. "Yes! Tonight! I fixed us dinner, and afterward I was going to tell you the whole story."

"Why didn't you tell me earlier?" His voice was too soft now.

"I tried. When we first met, I tried to tell you who I really was! I was—I was scared of losing you. Of what you would think of me. But this—" She almost gave way to tears but controlled her emotions with effort. "This is worse than anything I expected. Pierce, please—"

His face was in the shadows. She couldn't see him, and her instincts told her not to turn on the light. She watched him as he walked over to the heavy wooden desk at one end of the living room, couldn't stop looking at him as he opened the top drawer and extracted—

His checkbook.

"Let's finish this off, then, shall we?" When she didn't answer, he continued. "How much do you want for the rest of your performance? I believe Valerie said you needed the money—"

"No." Genie pushed a trembling hand through her hair. "Oh, no. Pierce, I never—"

He smiled, a tight ironic smile. "I said this to you once before. Don't do this."

She didn't want him to write her a check, didn't want things to degenerate to that point. "What do you want me to do?"

He left the checkbook on the desk and walked slowly over to the window. Folding his arms over his chest, he stared out into the night. When he finally spoke, his voice was so soft she barely heard him.

"I want you to get out."

AL DIDN'T SAY A WORD. He took one look at the expression on her face and simply held out his arms.

Genie went into them, but she didn't cry. After a second, she simply whispered, "It didn't go the way I thought it would."

"Do you want to talk about it?"

"No."

"I'll make up the couch."

He made her a cup of hot milk with cinnamon and simply sat next to her while it cooled on the coffee table. Then he brought out a pillow and blanket and made up the couch.

She didn't sleep. Instead, she reviewed the argument in her head throughout the long night.

What was he feeling right now? What was going through Pierce's mind?

Would she ever see him again?

PIERCE SAT QUIETLY in the chair by the window. He'd blown out the candles and left the lights off, except for one in the kitchen. The darkness suited his mood.

Why are you surprised? Everyone you've ever loved has always left. He took another sip of the drink in his hand, willing the alcohol to numb his brain, make things bearable.

This was different, and you know it. You pushed her out the door. He set the drink down on the small table by his chair and leaned back, closing his eyes.

Genie. Who was she, and why had she agreed to such a bizarre masquerade? Why hadn't Valerie wanted to do his show? Had it been some kind of sick game between the two of them?

As soon as the question formed in his brain he knew it wasn't true. Valerie had been surprised when he'd come around to her apartment. Genie hadn't known Valerie had lied.

It was confusing as all hell.

Who had she been in the bedroom? It had to be Genie. He doubted sleeping with him had been part of the job assignment. At least he *hoped* it hadn't.

He thought back to when he'd first seen her in New York, in front of the florist's. She wanted to tell him then, before they'd gone up to his apartment and made love. But he refused to talk, wanting only to feel her in his arms again.

And she had tried to tell him when he walked out of her suite in Chicago. It seemed like such a long time ago. She'd wanted to tell him before she left—he was sure of it.

At least you varied the pattern this time—made her walk out instead of you. Maybe it was for the best. He really wasn't very good at sustaining a relationship. If Genie was all she'd been at her best moments with him, she certainly deserved a man who was emotionally whole. Not a cripple.

He reached up and massaged the tense muscles at the back of his neck. *And you don't even know where she lives.*

He smiled grimly. One thing he knew for certain—Valerie wasn't going to tell him.

"DO YOU WANT any breakfast?" Al asked as Genie quietly folded up the afghan and placed the pillow on top of it. When she was finished, she sat back down on the couch.

"Not really."

"I'm making a cheese omelet. How about half?"

Knowing Al wouldn't give up, she nodded her head. Anything was better than sitting around feeling sorry for herself, Genie decided. She got up and followed Al into the kitchen. "I'll make hash browns." She knew Al liked the way she cooked potatoes. He always burned them, impatient to get to the final result.

Over breakfast Al asked, "So, what are your plans for today?"

"Nothing. I thought I'd go back to my apartment and see how the plants are doing."

"I'll go with you."

When they reached Genie's apartment, she did some superficial cleaning and talked with Al about meaningless things. All the while her mind was on Pierce.

What can I do to make things right?

"Genie?" Al gestured for her to sit on the sofa. "There's something I should have told you earlier."

She sat down next to him. "You're not to blame for any of this. It's my fault—"

He interrupted her. "After that last call of yours from Chicago, I started thinking about that article I read about Pierce's family. I didn't mean to butt in, but I went down to the library and looked through a stack of old magazines until I found it." He got up and walked over to his jacket and pulled out a wad of papers. "I copied the article. I should have given it to you before last night. It might have helped you."

Without another word he handed it to Genie, then sat down next to her.

She unfolded the creased pieces of paper. It looked

as if Al had been carrying them around in his pocket for a long time. Carefully smoothing them out, she began to read.

It was the story of a dynasty, but the human emotions involved were more painful than anything Genie had ever acted out on her soap. The article had obviously been the cover story, as almost seven pages were devoted to Pierce's family—how they had made their money, how they had used it, who had married whom and why.

Two-thirds of the way through the article, she stopped. Her eyes darted back, reread a paragraph. Reread it again. She closed her eyes tightly, her finger clutching the paper in her lap.

She felt Al's arm go around her shoulders. "Did he ever tell you about it?" he asked.

"No." Her voice was tight. Already Genie was imagining the pain Pierce must have gone through. "The only time he ever mentioned— He told me his mother left him her house when she died. He never told me how."

"It must have been a hell of a way to find out." When Genie remained silent, Al tried again. "What I meant was, I copied this article for you so that you would understand—"

"I know, Al. It's okay. It's just—" She set the article aside. "He was only around nine when it happened."

What had she been doing at nine? Val had been nineteen, constantly going out on dates. Genie could remember watching her get ready, wondering if she would ever look as beautiful. Looking down at her own flat chest, skinny legs and arms.

And her mother had always been there for her. For

each little bit of news. The school play. The newest book they had to read. The costumes that had to be made.

And she'd been there for the far more important questions. Do you like the way I am? Do you love me?

She began to read the article where she had left off. Forcing her eyes to keep moving over words. Simple black print on white paper. A record of a man's life.

And she remembered Pierce as she had first met him. The tightness around his mouth. His hesitant smile. The intense look in his eyes. How well he had learned about life. What horrible experiences it had given him.

She thought of the first time they'd made love. That morning in her suite. He had told her a little of his feelings then. *I've always thought of myself as—cold.* His experiences had given him good reason to freeze his feelings.

He'd opened up to her. Tears filled her eyes as she remembered his tone of voice that morning. *I've never been with any other woman the way I was with you.*

And she had taken his trust and destroyed it.

I can never give you the smallest amount of what you've given me. He'd come to care for her. Genie knew the depth of Pierce's emotional journey. It hadn't been easy for him, deciding to make love to a woman who was already married. She had wanted him so badly, cared so much, that her deception seemed small in comparison.

She'd only reinforced lessons he'd already learned. Love couldn't be trusted. Loss was to be expected.

Without meaning to, she had hurt him far more than she ever thought possible.

IT WAS the last thing he wanted to do, spend an evening with Barbara. But he'd promised. It wasn't every day she made a television appearance.

After Genie left, he went into the kitchen and checked the contents of the refrigerator. She'd been telling the truth about the dinner. The evidence was there, on pristine white plates. Perfectly sliced sirloin, scallions, ginger root. The wok was down off its hook, seasoned and set by the stove. All the utensils were neatly laid out on the counter. The spices had been taken off the rack.

I fixed us dinner, and afterward I was going to tell you the whole story.

He threw everything down the disposal, feeling sick to his stomach. Then he considered calling Valerie to get Genie's number. But after what he'd said to her at the party, he doubted she'd even speak to him.

The last thing he discovered was a small red lacquer box containing two fortune cookies. He took one out and crumbled it between his fingers. What kind of fortune would he have had tonight if he'd let her stay and explain?

He took the slip of paper and smoothed it onto the counter.

I'm sorry, Pierce.

Then the second cookie.

I love you.

He put both fortunes in the silver drawer and tossed the pieces down the disposal.

The buzzing doorbell brought him out of his thoughts, and when he answered, Barbara walked in, two brown bags in her arms.

"Did you remember to buy a tape?" she asked breathlessly.

"How could I forget when you called every hour?" *Don't ruin her moment with your unhappiness.*

As he programmed the videocassette recorder, his sister set out the Chinese food she'd brought. The row of white containers completely surrounded two paper plates.

"I brought your favorite. Beef in ginger sauce," Barbara said as she dished out their supper.

Within minutes, Barbara was watching the television intently, and Pierce was glad he didn't have to explain his lack of appetite. The beginning of "Entertainment Weekly," a magazine-format television show, flashed across the screen.

When Barbara's segment began, she screamed, then covered her mouth with her hand as she listened to herself explain the rigors of writing for a national soap opera. Pierce thought she came across as intelligent, sexy, knowledgeable and very human.

Her segment finished, and they raised their glasses, both filled with sake, to toast her television debut.

He moved to shut off the set, but Barbara stopped him.

"No, I want to see the rest. They're going to cover some of our rivals—the newer characters being developed."

When he saw Genie's face on the screen, he almost lost his dinner. It was her voice that caused him to snap his head around.

"How can you believe what she told you about me?" Her dark-brown eyes were filled with tears, her voice low and husky. "You know Margaret will do anything to get rid of me. But what hurts the most—" her dark eyes flashed defiantly "—what hurts the most is that you believed her!"

His eyes were riveted on the screen. Even as the scene began to unfold, Pierce felt a wild, primitive joy spread through his body. *He knew where to find her!*

The short interview with Genie fascinated him. It was as if he were meeting her for the first time. She was totally at ease, intelligent and funny. The camera loved her. Dressed in a short skirt, sweater and boots, she exuded a comfortable sexuality that was completely at odds with the way she'd portrayed her sister.

Pierce waited until the program was over, making sure Barbara saw everything she wanted to. Then he pounced.

"How can I meet Genie?" he demanded.

Barbara laughed. "I'm not sure that's part of my job assignment."

His impatience was almost palpable. "Help me out. Just this once."

"I've never seen you this interested in anyone! What about that girl friend of yours?"

Deciding it was time his sister knew, Pierce quickly told her the entire story.

Barbara sat quietly after he finished. "Will she want to see you again?"

"I'll *make* her happy to see me."

She tapped her fingernails on the surface of the inlaid coffee table. "There's a charity benefit this Friday night. All the actors and actresses from the soaps will be there." She grinned. "I need an escort—"

"You're on."

After Barbara left, Pierce picked up the living room, then rewound the tape and played it back. Genie fascinated him all over again. And he was going to see her. It didn't matter that he wasn't quite sure what he was going to say to her. He wasn't concerned with the fact that she might not want to talk to him.

For now, just seeing her would be enough.

"IT'S BEAUTIFUL ON YOU. That electric blue is your color."

Genie turned slowly in front of the three-way mirror. The dress sparkled as hundreds of tiny beads reflected the light, shimmering like moonlight on the water. When she moved, the beads created ripples over her figure.

"Give me just a moment longer." She smiled, softening her words. The saleslady bustled out of the dressing room.

Once she was gone, Genie carefully lowered herself into the solitary chair to see if she could sit down. Just barely. But the dress was so stunning it was worth the slight discomfort.

She wanted to look spectacular on Friday night. "It's not you they're coming to see," her agent had told her yesterday. "They want Joanna Morgan. See that you dress accordingly."

She stood up, then sat down again. This time it was easier. The dress was heavy, the weight of the beds tempting her to curve her shoulders.

But Joanna Morgan would never slump.

She walked slowly from one end of the large dressing room to the other, remembering when she'd been here with Valerie. It seemed so long ago. Then, she'd been intimidated, slightly awed by the elegance. Now she knew a little more about money and power.

What a fool she'd been to have believed money could solve any problem. Though she still had a healthy respect for being able to finance her career, she realized that all the money in the world couldn't buy back Pierce's trust. She couldn't wipe out the memory of his betrayed expression.

The saleslady knocked softly on the dressing-room door. "Can I help you with anything, my dear?"

Genie studied her reflection. She had to be ready for the benefit. And this dress did look like something Joanna would slink around in. It would go perfectly with the shoes she'd seen in the window at Saks.

"I'm just fine. It's a lovely dress, and I'm going to take it."

Chapter Eleven

"How do I look?" Genie stepped out of her bathroom and pirouetted in front of Al.

He let out a long, low whistle. "Like you're ready to steal a million hearts!"

"But do I look like Joanna Morgan?"

"Yep. She'd certainly wear a number like that."

"You look pretty terrific yourself." Genie made a minuscule adjustment to his black tie. "Thanks so much for going with me. It would have been awful to walk in alone."

"No problem."

"I'll try to introduce you to some people who can help you," Genie said as she walked over to the couch and picked up the long black velvet cape Valerie had lent her for the evening. Al was at her side in an instant, helping her slide her arms inside. Genie had styled her hair up so it wouldn't get tangled within the hundreds of tiny beads. Once the cape was on, the transformation was complete. She looked as Joanna would have looked if she were going to a party. The luxurious cape, the sensual beaded dress, the high-heeled silver shoes.

Perfect.

Picking up her evening bag, she walked out of the bedroom.

"COULD YOU HELP ME a minute, Barb?" Pierce frowned as he wrestled with a cuff link. Normally, he had no problem with the damn things. But tonight he felt full of nervous energy and his fingers just wouldn't obey. He let Barbara brush his hands aside and quickly complete the job.

"Thanks." His reply was gruff.

"You're welcome. Nervous?"

He nodded.

"Don't be. I'm sure as soon as you see her you'll think of the right thing to say."

He nodded again, not all that sure. But he wanted to start out, to move, to put his restlessness behind him. A man could worry himself to death.

"Let's go." He picked up his dinner jacket and put it on, then reached for his coat and gloves.

THE FORECOURT of the hotel was crowded with people. Bright lights were everywhere, some of them constant, some flashes from reporters' cameras. Genie watched the limousine ahead of them as the couple inside stepped onto the red carpet. Immediately bombarded with silver light, both actors posed for a second, then began their walk inside.

Al gave her arm a reassuring pat. "You'll be inside in no time."

"Do I look that scared?"

"Genie, just pretend you're Joanna. Give them a little bit of the show."

That did it for her. When her heels hit the red carpet, she *was* Joanna, all elegance and haughty grace. She smiled radiantly as cameras flashed and people cheered. Though her stomach was churning, her shoulders were straight, her posture perfect. The diamond-and-sapphire ring Valerie had lent her flashed as she waved.

Past the crowds, inside the hotel, she let out a long breath, then handed her cape to the hatcheck girl. "*That* was the most grueling thing I've been through all week." Tonight, Genie was determined to keep her thoughts of Pierce to a minimum. She was on the job tonight. Trying to keep things light, she looked up at Al and asked, "What if I'd tripped?"

"Don't think about it now. You didn't. It's over. Let's get a drink and check out the crowd."

Half an hour later, as Genie was listening to one of the producers discuss his latest project, she felt a peculiar tingling sensation wash up and down her spine. Someone was watching her. Though she disliked people who looked around while you talked to them, she did exactly that.

Pierce. She saw him immediately, looking supremely masculine in his tuxedo. His blue eyes were staring straight into hers. Her throat went dry, and she quickly diverted her attention back to the producer.

What was he doing here? How had he managed an invitation? What would she say if he wanted to talk to her? Questions raced frantically through her brain as she nodded and smiled to a group of actors passing by.

How can he look so terrific when I feel so terrible? Before her thought was fully formed, she answered her question. *He's over it.* The thought hit her like a blow, and she excused herself and headed for the opposite corner of the large ballroom. She had to get away.

Al. Al would know what to do. Perhaps she could just stay close to him, hide out, leave as soon as was decently possible. She knew she couldn't endure a long evening under Pierce's silent scrutiny.

She found Al within a minute. He was at the bar, talking to the bartender. Another actor of course.

"It's him. He's here," she whispered, accepting the glass of wine he passed to her.

"Pierce?" Al looked quickly around the room, spotted him, then turned back to Genie. "How did he get invited to this?"

"I don't know and I don't care," she lied, desperate to save what was left of her composure. "I just want to avoid him."

"That bad, huh?"

"What are you talking about?"

"You still love him," Al said softly.

"I detest the man." This was forced through gritted teeth. The auburn-haired casting director who had first auditioned Genie waved, and Genie waved back, forcing a smile.

"You'll probably have to talk to him sooner or later."

She took a large gulp of her wine. "Let's make it later. Much later."

PIERCE KEPT a careful eye on Genie from his corner of the room. Soon everyone would move into the dining room for dinner. But for now, he was simply content to watch her.

She was avoiding him, he was certain of that. He had seen the change come over her the moment she'd seen him. And he couldn't blame her.

He caught sight of Barbara as she wove her way

back toward him through the crowd. She was flushed and happy, stopping occasionally to chat or give someone a quick embrace. Pierce tried to control his steadily growing impatience. He wondered if she'd succeeded in switching the seating so he'd be next to Genie at dinner.

When Barbara was within six feet of him, she gave the tiniest, almost imperceptible shake of her head. Pierce frowned.

After she reached him, Barbara gave his hand a quick squeeze. "I couldn't do it. Genie—Joanna—is a very popular lady. You'll have to take your chances with her on the dance floor."

"WHO'S THAT BRUNETTE climbing all over him?" Genie had tried to remain cool and aloof. As usual, she was finding it totally impossible.

"I'm not sure, but we can find out," Al said. "Wait here."

When he got back, he handed her another glass of wine. "That's Barbara Stanton, head writer for 'Promise of Tomorrow.'"

His sister. Genie knew she was being childishly jealous, but the thought of Pierce with another woman upset her terribly. Even though he didn't want her, she couldn't bear the thought of him with another woman. He couldn't possibly be with anyone else the same way he had been with her. Images of Pierce in bed with her flashed through her mind: the strength of his body as he touched hers, the things he whispered to her as they made love. The soft kisses afterward, while she nestled in the crook of his arm.

Why was she even remembering? He'd made his opinion of her perfectly clear that night after the party.

Why did she have to go on torturing herself with memories?

It wasn't any of her business whom he chose to see.

"Looks like people are moving toward the dining room. Shall we?" Al offered her his arm.

"I'd be delighted." She'd have to really perform tonight, to hide her confusion and uncertainty. Pierce couldn't know how much she cared. With any luck, he'd thrown the fortune cookies away. She smiled up at Al, knowing she was being immature but hoping Pierce was watching them.

"WHO IS THAT GUY?" Pierce demanded, looking at the dark-haired man escorting Genie into the dining room.

"I'm not sure," Barbara murmured. "I've never seen him before."

As Pierce studied Genie and the man whose face she was smiling up into, he felt as if a red-hot poker were slowly being twisted inside him. He wondered if she would be going home with her escort tonight. Pierce remembered the way she responded in his bed, so warm and giving. The thought of her in another's man's arms was enough to make him want to tear through the sea of bodies between them and drag Genie all the way back to his apartment.

But she wasn't his partner tonight. He'd taken her feelings and thrown them away, made her leave his apartment. Hadn't even listened to what she had to say. It was his fault they weren't together tonight—his fault she was with that stranger.

"Pierce, you're hurting my arm."

Ashamed of his thoughts and the resulting action, he let go of Barbara, then looked down at the carpet for a second and took a deep breath. *Get control of yourself.*

Feeling totally vulnerable to his emotions, Pierce tucked his sister's hand into his arm and began to walk toward the dining room.

And Genie.

DINNER SEEMED to drag on forever. Normally Genie would have caught Al's eye and they would have had a private laugh over all the awards and speakers. Tonight it was too much of an effort. It was all she could do to keep her face carefully averted from the table Pierce was sitting at.

The procession of people up to the podium seemed to include just about everyone in the huge dining room. Al rolled his eyes at her once when a particular speech went on for over twenty minutes, but she barely smiled. How she wished Pierce was at the table with them. He would have laughed as well. She had loved making him laugh, wiping the lines of tension away from his mouth.

Genie sat very still, barely touching her food. Pierce was right behind her to her left. She kept her eyes strained straight ahead, not wanting to look at him. Throughout the presentation, she wondered why he was here.

Probably giving his sister support. It was just her bad luck she had to run into him.

When chairs around her were scraped back and people stood up and began to clap, Genie realized the banquet was over. As everyone began to file back into the ballroom, she wondered how soon she could politely make her escape.

PIERCE HAD WATCHED HER out of the corner of his eye throughout the banquet. She'd been the only thing that had relieved the monotony of the speakers. In front of him to his right, she'd been an easy target to pick out in that dress. He noticed every admiring male glance, and it had set his teeth on edge.

The orchestra was tuning up. Smiling tightly, he followed her into the ballroom, almost on the heels of her escort. What was he to Genie? He'd caught the way that guy had smiled at her, as if they were sharing a private joke. Had he pushed her back into an old lover's arms? Would she even want to talk to him? What if she refused to dance with him?

Pierce knew nothing was going to stop his pursuit. Now that they weren't sitting in predesignated seats, there would be no escape for her.

He wasn't sure what he was going to say. He only knew he had to talk to her, be close to her.

"DANCE WITH ME," Al whispered. "Here he comes."

She escaped out onto the dance floor with Al for a few seconds. When Pierce smoothly cut in, Al, to Genie's dismay, relinquished her.

They glided around the floor in silence. Genie barely missed a step. Pierce was an excellent dancer, but she'd suspected he would be. He did everything so well, why not this?

"Hello, Geneviève." His tone of voice gave her no clue as to what he was feeling.

"My name is Genie."

"Genie, then."

"Genie Hartley."

"Not Bouchet?" He seemed genuinely curious.

"No."

''Why not?''

She took a deep breath, trying to calm herself. ''I didn't want to trade in on my sister's success.''

''Okay, Genie.'' It sounded as if he was testing her name on his tongue. And liked it.

What now? she thought wildly as she felt his hand press insistently on the small of her back. His fingers were warm and firm. She could feel the warmth of his touch through the beads on her gown, and for one insane moment she wanted to melt into his arms and follow wherever he led.

''Who are you tonight?'' he asked quietly.

Stung, she almost stepped on his feet. ''I don't have to listen to any of your sarcastic remarks here—'' As she answered him, she looked up into his face. The expression in his eyes halted her angry outpouring of words.

His eyes were warm and caring. Soft and vulnerable. The way he'd looked after they'd first made love.

She drew in her breath sharply. What was he feeling? He couldn't be experiencing the same tumult she'd been facing since their argument. He'd been so quick to think the worst, not even willing to listen to her explanation.

''Who are you tonight? Really?'' He pressed her closer against him as the music slowed but continued. The lights had been lowered, and though Genie could hear people on the fringes of the dance floor talking and laughing, they sounded as if they were at the end of a deep tunnel. The only thing that mattered was that Pierce was holding her in his arms.

''Tonight? Joanna.'' She answered him without another second's hesitation. She would never lie to him again, especially if he gave her one more chance.

Pierce had been lied to all his life, if that article Al had given her had even been marginally accurate. She wasn't going to add to his disappointments.

He pressed his lips against her temple and she felt herself start to tremble.

"Pierce, don't—" she whispered brokenly.

"Lean on me. I'll hold you."

So she did. It felt wonderful, melting into his arms, letting him take the lead. He never directed them to the edge of the dance floor, never gave any other man a chance to cut in.

Genie closed her eyes as she rested her cheek against his jacket front. His touch brought back such sensual memories. Even if after tonight he never wanted to see her again, she would carry the memory of his touch with her for the rest of her life. Like being given another chance at heaven.

She wasn't sure when the music ended, but when Pierce stopped moving to the music, she opened her eyes and looked around the dance floor.

The crowd had thinned out. Most people had already left. She caught sight of Al, still waiting patiently by the bar, nursing a glass of wine.

Pierce ran a finger along her jawline, then tilted her face up to his. "Would you trust me enough to take a short walk with me?"

She laughed shakily. "Do you like me enough to want to take that walk?" She answered his question with the question that had been bothering her.

"I wouldn't ask if I didn't."

"Then my answer is yes."

She broke away from him long enough to go over and talk to Al. He was smiling as she explained, and

Genie was relieved he wasn't upset about her changing escorts in midstream.

"It was inevitable. That man isn't going to share you with anyone." He winked at her as he set his glass down on the bar. "You can get home all right, then?"

Strangely, she felt confident. She knew Pierce wouldn't hurt her. "I'm sure of it."

The streets were silent as they walked several blocks. Pierce put his arm around her shoulders, and Genie felt content to leave it there. Slowly, tentatively, as if she felt she almost didn't have the right, she slid her hand around his waist. Touching his body comforted her as they walked, his steps slower to make up for her shorter ones. The tight beaded skirt and high heels forced her to lean on him. She hadn't been planning on walking outside tonight.

"Do you mind going back to my apartment?" he asked.

She tensed for just a second, not sure whether she wanted to risk any intimacy with this man. Not just yet.

"I don't mean to bed. I mean to talk."

She took a deep breath of the cold winter air. "All right."

Inside the elevator she couldn't look at him. As he unlocked the door to his apartment, she watched the way his hand fumbled with the key. Knowing he was nervous reassured her.

Once inside, he lit the fire and poured two glasses of wine. She sat down on the edge of the couch and stared into the fire.

"Who are you now?" he asked.

"Genie," she said softly. "This is Genie." The words she'd longed to say the night of their argument came tumbling out. "I never meant to hurt you, Pierce. The whole thing was like—you know those snowballs in cartoons, the way they keep rolling and getting bigger and bigger? That's the way I felt about impersonating Valerie. But I never meant to hurt you. You have to believe that, even if you don't believe anything else."

"I know that now."

"What made you change your mind?"

He set his glass down and turned so he faced her, his arm resting along the back of the couch. He could easily have touched her, but he didn't. Genie was touched by his sensitivity to her feelings.

He didn't answer her question directly. "What made me most upset was I wasn't sure exactly who I had been close to. You or Valerie? But when I thought about it, nothing seemed to matter but finding you again and talking with you."

It was more than she had ever hoped for—another chance. "How did you know I would be at the hotel tonight?"

"I watched that television show last night. 'Entertainment Weekly.' Barbara was on, so I would have watched it anyway. I didn't know you were on at the end of it, but once I saw you it was easy to figure out which soap you were on. Then it was simply a matter of getting my sister to pull some strings."

"I'm glad she did."

She waited for him to speak again, and when he did, she sensed his reluctance. And knew whatever he was asking her cost him emotionally.

"When we—when you and I made love—"

She covered his hand with her own. "Maybe parts of the seduction were done as Valerie would have written them. But I was always myself when it mattered.''

He sighed, then rested his head in his hands. "I think that was what made me feel the worst. Thinking that you could have been pretending you were someone else at a moment like that.'' He studied her face, and the look in his eyes was so nakedly vulnerable she wanted to cry. ''I was hoping you weren't that good an actress.''

''Never. Please believe me.''

''Thank you, Genie.''

She owed him an apology. More than simply feeling she had to, she wanted to let him know how she felt. ''Pierce, I'm so sorry it happened. The more I got to know you, the more I wished—I wished we could have met somewhere besides the show. Then I thought about that, and I guess we wouldn't have met any other way. But I hated the deception from the first day, when I realized something was wrong.''

''Did Valerie simply send you out cold?''

Genie grimaced. ''She was eight months pregnant.'' At Pierce's look of surprise, she was astonished. ''She didn't tell you? Part of the reason I agreed to do it was that her doctor didn't want her to be under any pressure. She lost one baby before Kathryn, so she had to be very careful.''

''I didn't even know she had a child.''

''She kept it very quiet. Pierce, she's terrified of kidnapping. Valerie had a fan a few years back who followed her all over the city. She hung around in front of her old apartment, bothered her whenever she saw her. At first, Val gave her some books and talked with her. Later, it got so Val could barely go outside.

''When she and Harold first moved, they didn't give

their address out except to their closest friends and family. And her publicist.'' Genie stared into the fire, choosing her words carefully. ''I know there's nothing that can excuse what she did to your sister, but I understand Val's fears.''

Slowly he reached across the distance separating them and took her hand. The warmth from his fingers, the tightness of his grip, created a silent bond between them.

''I can understand fears like that. I know what it's like to be in the public eye.''

Genie held her breath, silently willing him to share his deepest tragedy with her.

But he didn't. He chose to change the subject. ''I was pompous, trying to play God. Barbara told me your sister was a blessing in disguise—Robert had been playing around for a long time before he met Valerie.''

Genie laid her head back against the couch and sighed. So it was all over, all their misunderstandings laid to rest. But her fears were still there. Would Pierce care for her once he got to know her? A part of her knew the woman he had cared for, had followed to New York, was simply herself. But did he know that? Did he want to try again?

She didn't want to speculate alone. ''Where does that leave us?'' she asked softly.

''I'd like to try again. But I'd like us to start over, get to know each other again. I don't know much about you, Genie. I have no idea of who you are, what you want.'' He let go of her hand and leaned forward, framing her face in his fingers. ''But I want to know you.''

It would have to be enough. Sensing he wasn't going to push her physically, Genie leaned forward and kissed him. His hands moved to her waist, resting gently against her body. There was no pressure, no demand. It was a first kiss—the first time he'd kissed her knowing she was Genie.

When they broke apart, he leaned back on the couch. "So what do actors like to do in their spare time?"

She smiled. "This actor barely has any. But when I do..." She thought for a minute. "I like to see foreign films."

His eyes lit up. "I love them. Would you like to go out tomorrow night?" He was endearingly formal, asking her out for the first time. Genie loved him for it.

"How about the twenty-third?" she asked, naming the day after tomorrow. "There's something I have to clear up first."

"It's a date." He rose from the couch. "I'll see you home."

"Just see me to a taxi, and I can get home fine." She was suddenly self-conscious about where she lived. Pierce was used to elegance—her studio seemed shabby when she saw it through his eyes. Her hectic schedule had kept her too busy to think about moving. And in some ways, despite its crowded interior, she loved her little studio.

"Sure?" His eyes were darkly questioning.

She nodded her head.

Before she stepped inside the cab, Pierce made final arrangements. "I'll pick you up. Where do you live?"

"I'll meet you here," she answered quickly. "Is six okay?"

"Perfect. We'll get something to eat."

She watched him through the back window until the cab rounded a corner, then turned around and faced front.

It's a start. At least he's willing to give me another chance. But I wonder if he'll ever trust me enough to tell me everything.

Chapter Twelve

"Geneviève!" Valerie waved her elegantly manicured fingertips in the air, in a classic gesture Genie had seen many times. "You can't be serious!"

"I am." Genie leaned forward so her face was inches away from her older sister's and spoke very softly, emphasizing each word. "What's done is done. I can't change the past. But I'm going to make sure my future is different."

"Genie, I've never seen you this way." Valerie avoided her eyes, then picked up her fork and took another bite of her strawberry crepe.

"That's because I never had the courage to stand up to you, Val, I've been doing your dirty work for as long as I can remember. How about the time you sent me over to return those library books? They were all overdue, and I lost my entire allowance paying your fines."

"Oh, for God's sake, Genie, are you going to rehash our entire childhood? Was that the purpose of this dinner?"

"No. Val, this last time—doing that talk show—I finally recognized the pattern you and I have fallen into. And I'm not happy with it. Let's just say this invitation was extended so I could give you fair warning. I'm putting you on notice. I'm not available to do anything for you, except baby-sit Kathryn. And that's only because I want to."

Valerie's sensual mouth took on a decided pout. "Genie! You're so boring this way! Besides, if it weren't for the money I paid you, you would have never gotten your part on 'Malibu's—'"

"No, Val. That I got for myself. That was my hard work alone—you can't take any of the credit."

Valerie sulked silently. Then, as if remembering her facial expression would encourage wrinkles, she relaxed her face into a deceptively serene expression. And Genie sensed the final test had come.

"Actually, darling, there was another reason I accepted this dinner invitation. You see, my publicist wants me to attend a book signing the second week in January, and it's just that—well, you know Kathryn hasn't let me sleep a full night since we came home from the hospital and my skin looks dreadful. Anyway, I was hoping—"

"No." Genie spoke the single word from a deep sense of personal conviction. It was easier than she'd expected. Valerie hadn't been listening to a word she'd been saying! How well she'd anticipated her sister.

"But, Genie—"

"Cancel it." Genie picked up her wineglass. "Read my lips, Val. Never again."

It was the first time she'd ever seen her older sister at a loss for words. Genie decided to take advantage of it, sensing she wouldn't be seeing Valerie for a few weeks at least. Until she cooled off.

"Here's to the new me! I'm giving you warning, Val. Don't try to manipulate me anymore."

When her sister still didn't reply, she decided to drop her final bombshell. "Why didn't you tell me Pierce came to your apartment?"

"He told you?" Valerie was aghast, her face quickly turning a pale shade of green. She didn't look too serene now.

"Yes. Val, I want you to see what you did in terms of how it affected people besides yourself. So you got your interview. Big deal. You could have put the whole thing off until after Kathryn was born—"

"But the book was being shipped!" Valerie wailed. "Genie, you know how you have to time these things!"

"There are more important things in life besides publicity. You *hurt* me. And you hurt Pierce. You played everyone against the middle, hoping no one would ever find out. So you'd come out on top. It's the only thing I don't like about you."

"Is he going to—now that he knows, is he going to—" Val broke off, speechless.

"I don't know what he's going to do. But I'd think about it, the next time you decide to dabble in other people's lives."

Valerie looked as if she'd had quite enough of the conversation. She grabbed her purse, fumbling for her wallet. Genie reached out quickly and covered her sister's trembling hand.

"I've put dinner on my card, Val. I just want you to think about what I said, okay?"

Her sister stilled her nervous movements.

"I'd like to get to know you all over again, too, Val."

LATER THAT NIGHT in her studio, Genie thought back over the week. So much had happened. Had it been only five weeks since she'd first met Pierce? How was it possible her life had changed so quickly?

She picked up the cup of warm milk on the kitchen counter, then padded barefoot to the overstuffed chair by the window and sat down. Staring out the window into the darkness, she could barely see the fire escape beyond, or the naked branches of the oak tree outside in the courtyard below.

What was he doing right now? What was he thinking? Pierce was a man who held his emotions exquisitely in check. She was able to read a few feelings in his face, but he kept so much inside him.

As her thoughts skipped back to the article Al had given her, she set her cup down. It hurt to think of what he'd been through.

Suicide. Even at her worst moments, Genie had never considered taking her own life. Though after reading this history of Pierce's family, she could understand what had driven his mother.

To understand that at the age of nine. She couldn't conceive of it. And he hadn't even been told by his family. His mother's death had been an "accident." Until Pierce had found out at his boarding school.

One of the men who'd been interviewed for the article had gone to boarding school with Pierce. They'd been playing soccer that day. A teammate had given Pierce a clipping from a Chicago newspaper. It contained the truth about his mother's death. Pierce had started running, running toward the forest on the edge of the playing field. When they'd found him, he'd been silently crying, rubbing the blood off his face. He'd run until he'd fallen, then lay on the ground and cried.

When she thought of him, so small and alone with his pain, Genie wanted to pick up the phone and call him. She wanted to talk with him, let him know she was here for him. For anything.

But this wasn't the sort of confidence you took from a person, emotional pain like this. It had to be something freely given, something willingly shared. Thank God he'd had Barbara. Yet she'd been only thirteen when she lost her mother. How much could she have helped Pierce through his pain?

Patience was not one of Genie's foremost qualities. More than anything, she wanted to be able to see three months into the future, see where her relationship with Pierce was headed. Was he even capable of maintaining an emotional relationship with a woman?

So much of his emotions surfaced when they made love. Perhaps it was because the bedroom was the only place he felt safe with his feelings.

She picked up her milk. It was lukewarm, but she drank it anyway, resisting the temptation to call him. They both needed time. She'd see him tomorrow, have dinner with him, enjoy a movie.

She'd have to wait as patiently as she could for the future.

REMEMBERING THEIR FIRST DINNER, Genie decided on pizza. She and Pierce took the subway to Little Italy, where they sat in a café for two hours, drinking wine and eating dinner. By the time they left and started walking toward the movie theater, it had begun to snow.

He held her against him with his arm, steadying her when she skidded on the ice. They walked slowly, not rushed for time.

Standing in line for the movie, Genie tried to keep their conversation light and funny. She wanted to make him laugh. Pierce was impressed and amused by the stories she told him about her job, from antics on the set to the exhausting chore of learning twenty-five pages of dialogue in a single night.

They were almost at the ticket booth when a woman's voice made Genie turn.

"Joanna Morgan?"

Someone had recognized her from the show. This was another first in Genie's life, so she smiled at the woman.

"Yes, I am."

She was totally unprepared for the woman's assault.

"You lying little bitch!" Her face twisted into a vicious grimace. "I've seen the way you treat Jared!" The woman raised her bulky handbag into the air and brought it down over Genie, all her fury behind the attack. "And Margaret! The way that poor woman takes abuse from you!" She raised her bag again, pure hatred in her eyes.

Pierce moved quickly. Genie felt his hands grasp her shoulders, then he pinned her to the wall of the theater, his body shielding her from the woman's attack. She could feel him tense as the bag hit his body. Their attacker was so immersed in her fury she didn't seem to care whom she was hurting.

"Lying little—scheming bitch!" People in line were stepping back, out of harm's way. Still Pierce protected her, angling his body so the woman couldn't get at Genie no matter how hard she tried.

Genie clutched the front of Pierce's jacket, holding on to him in her fear. The woman's attack had taken her completely by surprise. She hid her face in his chest and winced each time she felt his body tense, as if she felt each blow he received.

She heard a commotion, then two of the ushers came out and took hold of the woman. She screeched as they pulled her away, babbling nonsensical words.

Her composure totally shattered, Genie kept her face turned against Pierce's chest as he led her out of the line, past curious eyes. When he reached the curb, she felt him raise his arm to hail a cab.

"Genie, are you all right?"

She nodded into his chest. "I want to go home."

He gave the driver his address.

She broke down in the cab, and he pulled her into his lap, cradling her against the hard warmth of his body. When they reached his apartment, he carried her inside and into the elevator. Not until he shut his apartment door behind them did he finally set her down.

He sat with her on the couch, handing her tissues, letting her cry out her fears, both for herself and for him.

"Pierce, she hurt you! Take off your shirt and let me see your back."

His beautiful muscled back was mottled with the beginnings of black-and-blue marks. Genie traced her fingers gently over his skin.

"Do you have an ice pack? If I get some ice on this, it won't hurt as much."

She made him lie down on the couch as she found the bag and filled it with ice. Genie patted it very gently over his back, hoping to ease the soreness.

Once she was certain his needs had been taken care of, she asked the question haunting her. "Why did she do that? How could she think I was really Joanna?"

"She was crazy, Genie. She had to be." Pierce

spoke quietly, his head resting on his arms. Then, very slowly, he sat up and pulled her back into his lap, wrapping his arms around her.

She tried to get up, but he held her tightly. "Don't leave unless you want to."

"But I'm too heavy," she protested weakly.

"Never."

She buried her face against his neck, too tired to move.

She wasn't sure how much later it was in the evening when Pierce got up, lifting her gently in his arms. He carried her into the bedroom and set her down on the bed. Carefully, as if she were made of porcelain, he undressed her and tucked her beneath the sheets.

Exhausted, Genie turned her face into the pillow and slept.

EARLY IN THE MORNING, she woke up. For a second she didn't know where she was. Then she remembered. Turning her head slightly, she saw Pierce lying in bed beside her.

He looked exhausted, as if he'd been fighting an inner war. She remembered the last time she'd watched him sleep, how relaxed he looked. Now it seemed something was haunting him.

She closed her eyes again, wondering what they would talk about when they were both awake. She opened her eyes and glanced at the window behind her head. Snow still continued to fall, lightly tapping against the panes of glass.

More than anything, she wanted to slide over against Pierce and wrap her arms around him. But she didn't really have that right. She was in his bed because of what had happened last night. He had taken care of her the way he would have looked after a frightened child.

The mattress moved beneath her and she glanced over at him. His forehead was tense, as if he were deep in thought. Then his lips moved, and Genie recognized a single word.

"No." It came out a soft moan.

She almost touched him but drew her hand back. She didn't want to scare him.

He moved again, more restlessly this time. Perspiration beaded his forehead. Was he sick?

With a suddenness that almost threw her off the mattress, he jackknifed up into a sitting position. "No!" He shouted this time, his voice loud and agonized in the silent apartment.

Pierce covered his face with his hands. As Genie wrapped her arms around him, his shoulders started to tremble. She kissed the back of his neck, stroked his hair. She knew what was riding him, what had come to him during the night and given him this nightmare. More than anything, she wanted to give him reassurance and strength from her body. Peace.

"Pierce?" Her voice was soft. Unsure.

He surprised her then, turning to her just as she thought he would push her away, taking her in his arms and holding her very tightly as he lay back against the mattress. His entire body was shaking. She held on to him, letting the tremors pass into her body, trying to absorb some of his pain.

Their bodies were pressed tightly together, and Genie could feel the damp coolness of his. She wrapped her legs around him, willing some of her warmth into his body.

Slowly, very slowly, he quieted. As his body began

to warm, as his trembling subsided, she held him against her heart, murmuring nonsensical words and stroking his brow. The same words her mother had used when she herself sometimes woke up from a bad dream.

Then he buried his face against her shoulder, and it was several minutes before she realized her skin was wet. He'd been lying so very still. Genie felt him take one long, shuddering breath. Then another. She stroked his hair gently as he began to sob.

SHE WOKE as she felt him move away from her.

"Pierce?" Her voice was thick with sleep.

"I'm all right."

She sat up then, pushing her hair out of her eyes. His back was turned toward her as he slipped on a pair of jeans.

"I'm sorry you had to be—bothered." This was the voice of a stranger. Not Pierce.

Genie chose her words carefully, knowing he was especially vulnerable. "You didn't bother me, Pierce."

He was pulling on a sweater, then turned to face her but didn't meet her eyes. "I suppose you should be going home."

He wanted her to go. She could see it in the uncomfortable set of his shoulders, in his abrupt tone. He didn't want her close to him.

Why can't we talk about this? But even as she thought the words, she knew they wouldn't talk.

"I'll be ready in five minutes," she said brightly, forcing herself to be cheerful. To ignore the pain twisting her insides. How could they hope to have a relationship if he couldn't talk about the most important feelings he had?

Genie was silent as they descended in the elevator and as Pierce hailed a cab. Sliding inside, she resisted the urge to ask when she'd see him again.

She didn't want to know the answer.

BE A LITTLE MAN.

How he'd hated those words. Pierce lay in the darkened bedroom watching the snowflakes float gently by the window. He'd sent Genie away almost five hours ago, yet he couldn't stop thinking about her.

He'd had the nightmare before. With other women in his bed. Without exception, they'd shrunk from him, seemed astonished that a man with his control could break down.

It seemed such a simple concept to understand: the tighter the control, the stronger the emotions.

They had wanted him to be strong for them but hadn't wanted to give anything in return.

Except for Genie.

It must have been frightening for her. He knew he had screamed as he sat up in bed.

No. He'd screamed the same word when he first saw the clipping. And if it had been deeply embarrassing to display emotion to the women who had shared his bed, it had been doubly unforgivable to break down in front of the boys he went to school with.

So he had run away.

He shifted his body, got up off the bed, and walked into the living room. She'd wanted to stay with him. She loved him.

And she deserved better than he could ever give her.

He had avoided asking himself so many questions.

Afraid of the answers. But tonight something inside him had been opened up.

No, you're still lying to yourself. It didn't just suddenly happen tonight. It began to happen when you first met her.

Genie did funny things to his emotions. He started dreaming frequently. Remembering painful incidents. She seemed to open him up effortlessly, and he wasn't sure he liked the feeling.

Be a little man. His father had said those words at his mother's funeral. So he forced himself to stare dry-eyed at her coffin. He could still remember the scent of hundreds of flowers, including the blanket of white roses over her casket. To this day, the smell of roses made him sick.

After his mother's death, he'd been shunted around to different relatives when the various boarding schools closed for the holidays. His father had been too busy—or unable—to deal with the little boy who looked so much like his dead wife.

Later on, as he got older, he chose to remain at school over the holidays. Anything was preferable to being with people who made it so carefully, politely clear they didn't want you.

He'd chased after so many of the things guaranteed to bring him happiness. The job. Women. Cars. Expensive vacations. Nothing had filled the emptiness.

Until the first night he spent with Genie. He woke up that morning scared of the intensity of his feelings. Almost relieved she was married. He could still remember the agonized look on her face, the way she'd begged him to stay.

But he'd run. Run back to a job that was dissatisfying, to a life that seemed colorless and cold without her.

Nothing had been the same after meeting her. It had been the beginning of the end of fooling himself. So he quit his job. He looked for her. When he found her again, he felt that same sense of peace. Until he found out about the masquerade.

Then you couldn't wait to push her out the door. He hadn't listened to her, hadn't even tried to understand. But the minute she walked out the door, he started missing her.

And he'd done the same thing tonight.

So you have a choice. To go on as you always have, or… To find Genie. To talk to her, try to explain how terrifying it was to face feelings that had been buried for years.

He went into the kitchen and turned on the light, determined to settle in for the night and forget. Opening the refrigerator door, he poured himself a glass of wine and walked back into the living room. Once he settled himself in the chair, he stared out the window, preparing himself for another solitary evening.

But it wasn't working this time. He couldn't stop thinking about her. Christmas Eve. Would Genie be with her family? Would she think of him? Barbara had flown to the West Coast to be with a man she'd been seeing for the past three years. Pierce had assured her he'd be fine. What was one more holiday by himself?

Break the chain. You can do it. With slow, precise movements, he set the glass down on a small table and walked back toward the front door, reaching for his overcoat.

Chapter Thirteen

"Hello, Valerie," Pierce said as she swung open the door.

"What are you doing here?" she said, glancing back over her shoulder. She was obviously in the middle of a dinner party. Her hair was waved becomingly around her face, and the long red velvet dress looked festive as it clung to the full curves of her figure.

"I'm here to get Genie's address." He'd been halfway down the elevator when he realized he didn't know where she lived. But he knew who did. And she was going to tell him.

"I'm not sure I should give you Genie's address," Valerie said quietly, glancing over her shoulder again.

"Valerie, who is it?" That had to be Harold.

"Just a friend of Genie's," she replied quickly. Turning back toward him, she hissed, "You have to leave before my husband sees you! He'll know you know I never did your show!"

"Valerie," said Pierce slowly, enjoying each second of her squirming, "let's make a deal. I know how much you enjoy making deals."

"Oh, stop making fun of me and tell me what you want!" she snapped.

"I'll get straight to the point. Either you give me your sister's correct address or you'll have a major lawsuit on your hands. How does that sound?"

He watched as her face turned pale, as she reached up and touched her throat with a shaking hand. "Lawsuit?"

"You agreed to appear on my show—not to send someone else."

Her eyes narrowed. *Always looking for a deal,* Pierce thought quickly. Valerie was one woman he hoped he'd never have to be up against again.

"And if I give you her address, will you leave me alone?"

"You have my word." He could barely keep a straight face at the look she shot him.

"Let me get a piece of paper."

Within minutes he was out on the street, hailing a cab.

"DID YOU STICK those cookies in your bag?" Genie asked Al as he began to rearrange things in his small suitcase.

"Yes. When do you leave for your mother's?"

"In the morning. I'm taking the train at seven."

"You won't be lonely?" Al asked pointedly.

"No. I—I need the time to think."

"He'll come around. I'll call you Christmas Day, okay?"

"Okay."

He wrapped his arms around her and gave her a fierce hug. Genie hugged back, thankful Al was so understanding. She wanted to be alone tonight.

As he picked up his suitcase and opened the door, she said softly, "Don't let your dad get you down, Al. I know your break is just around the corner."

"Hey, I'll be okay. It was almost as good when you got Joanna. My two older brothers can't wait to meet you."

"I'll bet. You be careful, Al. If you're not back by New Year's, I'm coming to Brooklyn to get you!"

Laughing, he walked out into the hall and began to clump down the stairs in his boots.

After he left, she went back into the kitchen and checked the timer on the stove. The sugar cookies were ready to come out. Grabbing a pot holder, she eased the hot cookie sheet out of the oven and inserted a second one. She put the cookies on some of the brown bags that lay flattened on the table and left the hot sheet on the counter to cool.

She was slicing the rolled-up dough when she heard a knock on the door.

Al. He'd never made it out her door without coming back at least once.

"Did you forget something?" she said as she swung open the door. Her laughter died in her throat as she looked up at Pierce.

His expression was serious. "Yes, I almost did." His arms were weighted down with brown paper bags. Genie recognized the smell of Chinese food. Ginger beef. Chaplin jumped down from his cushion on the couch and began to dance around their legs, bouncing and barking furiously.

"I think I caused us to miss this dinner once before, so I thought I'd bring it to you."

She couldn't reply, her throat was so tight.

"Genie, are you okay? Am I—"

"No, come in. I'll get some plates. Chaplin, stop! This is Pierce."

She was touched by the way he knelt down and held out his hand to her dog. Chaplin came slowly forward, sniffed cautiously, then let Pierce scratch his head. Soon the little dog was licking his fingers.

As she was searching through her cupboards for plates, the timer went off with a sharp ping.

"Can you just pull those cookies out? I was baking for tomorrow's party."

He took the sheet out of the oven and slid another one in. She watched him as he studied her small kitchen, a mixture of hanging plants, framed theater posters, an extensive spice rack and pots hung from a pegboard on the wall. The red gingham curtains she'd made were slightly crooked, but the geraniums by the window were full and bushy.

"It looks like you."

Why had she been reluctant for him to see where she lived? He fit right in.

She climbed up on top of the computer to search for the paper plates in the top cupboard, then gasped as she felt his hand close over her ankle.

"Get down from there. Tell me what you're looking for and I'll take a look."

It was easier for Pierce, since he only had to stand on the step stool. Genie couldn't take her eyes off him as he rummaged through the shelves, finally producing the paper plates.

They ate in the kitchen, Chaplin sitting beneath her chair and begging for scraps. As Genie picked at her ginger beef, she wondered what Pierce was going to say. Was this his way of telling her he wanted to see her again? Or was he going to ask if they could be just friends? She didn't think she could bear that.

She cleared away the plates, and Pierce leaned back in his chair. He seemed uneasy. Tense.

"Don't clean up now. Come here."

She sat down again across from him. He still seemed nervous.

"You didn't open your fortune cookie," he said. "I looked all over the city for a restaurant that was still open." As he spoke, he opened another little paper container and handed it to her.

She took the cookie on top. "You take one, too."

He shook his head. "Uh-uh. These are both for you."

Her heartbeat started to drum crazily as she snapped the delicate cookie in half. Pulling out the thin strip of paper, she turned it over.

I love you, Genie. The hand-printed message swam in front of her eyes. When she looked up at him, he was smiling.

"I love you, too," she whispered.

"The second one's yours also." He handed her the box.

She opened it more slowly this time, emotion making her clumsy. Her hands shook as she smoothed out the second paper fortune beside the first.

Will you marry me?

Unable to speak, she nodded her head. He leaned across the table and kissed her.

"I missed you." His whispered words were almost lost as he stood up, closed his fingers gently over her wrist, and pulled her into his arms. He buried his face in her hair and held her tightly.

A few minutes later he began to walk. First to the

light switch in the kitchen, which he turned off. Then to the oven.

Then to the main room, where the loft bed stood solidly in one corner. He let go of her long enough for both of them to climb up, the mattress squeaking gently as he relaxed against her.

There were no lights on, and when he reached for her bedside lamp, Genie placed a hand on his arm.

"No, let's leave it off." She didn't want anything to disturb the warm cocoon of sensation beginning to build around them. She sighed with contentment as he took her in his arms, as his lips covered hers, teasing and caressing. It was as exciting as the first time. Because he knew her. Knew that when he kissed the side of her neck, it caused her heart to hammer furiously. He knew she liked the softest of touches on her breasts with his hands, but not with his mouth. He knew she wanted to be brought along slowly, savoring each moment.

And she knew him. She recognized by the slight trembling of his body how much sensual energy was held in check. Knew by his touch, his kiss, that he loved her. It was so much more than a promise of marriage. It was a feeling, an instinct. He would always be sensitive, as kind as he knew how.

She touched him carefully at first, her hands remembering the feel of his smooth, hard muscles, the way his skin always seemed hot to her touch. As she rolled over on her back and cradled him gently between her thighs, she could feel his excitement and she parted her legs, pressed gently on the small of his back so he would be closer to her. The roughness of his chest hair against her breasts caused her nipples to tighten in almost painful anticipation. She had never wanted any man the way she wanted him. Would always want him.

When he lowered his mouth to one of her breasts, she cried out softly. Shafts of intense pleasure seemed to splinter inside her, warming her blood, making her thighs soft and fluid. She wrapped her legs tightly around him, tried to slow him, but he continued his exploration of her body. A sensual weakness washed over her as his mouth moved to her other breast, then down her stomach to where sensation was most intense.

He held her thighs gently apart, and she groaned as his tongue flicked out, touching her intimately. She was beyond any conscious control. Her hands moved down and she shaped them to his head, touching him blindly. He moved his hands under her hips, guiding her movements until her arousal was a tight, sharply stretched feeling.

Her body felt as if it were snapping, the tenuous thread of control completely destroyed. Genie bit down on her lip, turned her head into the pillow, groaned deeply as she found release from a tension that had been building since the last time Pierce had made love to her.

He lay with his head against the softness of her thigh as her breathing returned to normal. One of his hands was curled lightly over her breast, and it felt to Genie as if her heart were beating so strongly it was pouring into his body. She lay perfectly still, wanting to please him but not able to lift her body out of bed.

It was several minutes before she could speak.

"Pierce?"

"Hmmm?" He slid up beside her and put an arm

around her shoulder, then pillowed her head against his chest.

"Come here." She reached for his hip, pulled on it gently.

"Rest a little more," he whispered as he smoothed a damp strand of hair away from her forehead.

She caught his hand and kissed it, then placed it over her breast. Sliding her hand underneath the covers, she touched his stomach, then moved lower until she found him, still intensely aroused. She touched the hot smooth skin slowly, knowing he was enjoying what she was doing to him.

Genie slid to her side, her hand never leaving him. She moved her body until her lips were level with his ear. "I need you." Her lips trembled as she took a breath. "I need you very much."

His movements were so sudden, so fluid that they took her by surprise. Within seconds she was on her back. He pushed her knees up gently and entered her, his strokes powerful. Her breath caught; then she cried out with pleasure as he took her, filling her with the full length of his masculine arousal. The center of all sensation focused on where their bodies were joined, where they became one.

She could feel he was holding back, waiting for her, and she didn't want him to. She wanted to be caught up in a blaze of desire, wanted his excitement to add to hers.

His breath was hot against the side of her neck, his stomach smooth and hard as it moved against hers in an undulating, sensual rhythm. She felt him grow even harder inside her; then his entire body stiffened. Genie felt his small contractions, and it was just enough to trigger her own response. She held him tightly, closed her eyes and rode a passion that rocked her body, caused every inch of her to tremble.

Several minutes later she reached her hand up and softly threaded her fingers through his hair. It was damp, and she moved her fingers to his face, smoothing the hair off his high finely-shaped forehead.

Her sense of possession was sweet and intense. They belonged to each other now, had gone through so much to arrive at this place.

He moved slightly, so that his face rested against her breasts. His breath tickled her; it was warm and soft against her skin. She continued to play with his hair almost absently.

"I take it the answer is still yes?" His voice was so soft she barely heard it. There was just the faintest amusement in his tone.

She began to laugh, from deep inside. How she loved this man! Her fingers pulled slightly at his hair, so he had to look up and see her eyes.

"What would you do if the answer was no?" She couldn't resist teasing him.

He moved quickly, pinning her hands on either side, his body over hers. "I'd tie you up and tickle you—I've have to start convincing you all over again."

She could barely talk, she was laughing so hard. "I just need a little more time to think—"

He dipped his head slightly, and she felt his lips close over her breast, tender from their lovemaking.

"Don't!" The sensation was too intense.

He stopped, but only for a second. "The lady said she needed more convincing."

"She was lying! She was lying!" She could feel him nudging her thighs apart, and when he lowered his body between her legs, she looked up at him in shock.

"I can't believe—"

"Believe it," he said firmly as he slowly moved inside her and captured her heart all over again.

MUCH LATER that evening they lay in the loft bed. Snow was still falling, and Genie had turned on the clock radio to keep track of the weather.

"We might be snowed in tomorrow," she said, snuggling closer against him.

"Would you mind?" He kissed her shoulder, and the feel of his lips on her skin made her stomach contract.

"No." She traced her finger along his chest, around his collarbone. "I can't think of anyone I'd rather be trapped with."

They watched the snow for several minutes, then Pierce said quietly, "I'm sorry I made you leave this morning."

She moved so her head was cradled on his chest. "But you came back. That's all that matters."

He closed his eyes and sighed deeply.

"Pierce?"

"Hmmm?" He sounded deeply content.

"Will you tell me about it someday?"

Slowly he nodded his head.

She kissed his neck. Suspecting he'd had very few happy Christmases, she decided to change the subject. "Could you do one more thing for me?"

"Whatever you want."

Turning toward him, she whispered into his ear.

Smiling, he rolled over so his hips pinned hers

against the mattress. "Where did you come up with that? That's wilder than anything in Valerie's books."

She shut her eyes and smiled as laughter bubbled up inside her. "But you're the only man I've ever thought about doing it with."

Slowly, very slowly, he reached over and shut off the radio. "Your imagination, Geneviève, never fails to astound me."

As he kissed her cheek, she whispered, "I have enough crazy things thought up to keep us entertained forever."

"You do, huh?" He kissed her temple, then her ear. "I guess I'm going to be a very busy man."

"Oh, only for the rest of your life," she whispered.

"Sounds fine to me," he said, then gave her a playful swat on her bottom. "Now stop talking and start doing."

Epilogue

"He's seven pounds eleven ounces, twenty-two inches long." Pierce's voice was full of pride as he spoke to Genie's mother over the phone. "I don't know who he looks like. Genie says he has my eyes, but the nurse told me all babies are blue-eyed at birth." He smiled. "Besides, I think she's prejudiced."

He listened to his mother-in-law's concerned advice, then said softly, "I'll tell her that. She's asleep right now, but I'll let her know as soon as she wakes up." The last words of the conversation came easily to him. "I love you too, Mom, and I'll take good care of her."

He hung up the pay phone and started down the hospital hall. One of the maternity nurses caught his eye and smiled reassuringly.

"They're both fast asleep, Mr. Stanton, and doing fine."

He nodded, not trusting himself to continue talking. The last twenty-three hours, culminating in the birth of his son, had been exhausting. Genie had insisted on natural childbirth, so he'd attended all the classes and coached her through the entire delivery.

If he thought she was a brave woman for marrying

him, it was nothing compared to what he'd seen her go through yesterday. Deep inside, he was afraid of losing her, but he concentrated on breathing with her, wiping her forehead, telling her where she was in the course of the delivery.

At the end the doctor asked him if he wanted to catch the baby. Pierce saw his son come into the world, was the first to hold him. He was moved deeply by the expression on Genie's face when their child was put in her arms, and any lingering doubts as to whether they were doing the right thing were banished.

Since Genie had insisted on natural childbirth, he'd insisted on rooming in—for both father and child. Though the hospital hadn't been as receptive as he would have liked, in the end he triumphed. Pierce wasn't going to go home to their empty apartment.

He walked quietly into their room and shut the door behind him. As he looked down on the two sleeping figures in bed, he smiled.

Genie had taken the baby out of his bassinet and taken him to bed with her, putting him close to her breasts. She looked totally exhausted, and her face was turned into the pillow in a way familiar to him.

Taking off his shoes, Pierce eased himself down on the bed, careful not to jostle either his wife or son. He leaned back against the bedframe, sitting up slightly.

Eight years. Eight years since he'd stopped running, since the night he'd gone to her studio apartment with Chinese food. It had become a private family tradition—Chinese food and fortune cookies on Christmas Eve. The fortunes inside had changed slightly throughout the years, but never the feeling behind them.

At his insistence they lived together for six months before they married. He wanted to make sure Genie knew what she was getting into. And on their wedding day, in front of her family and Barbara, she looked at him as if to say, ''Silly! I knew all along this would work.''

The miracle was that it had.

He'd decided to return to the business world as Genie's manager. He had gone back to law school at the age of thirty-five and had graduated from Harvard with honors. Now he looked over every contract she signed. He also maintained a small private practice. And at least he felt he was doing something worthwhile—changing people's lives.

Genie had moved from ''Malibu's Children'' to feature films after years of hard work. Last year she'd been nominated for an Academy Award and though she hadn't won, he had the fun of flying her out to Los Angeles and renting a suite for her at the Beverly Wilshire. On the way to the Dorothy Chandler Pavilion in their rented limousine, she turned to him and said that no matter what happened that night, she wanted to get pregnant before the year was out. Though she joked about the advanced age of her eggs, he knew she was serious.

He'd had his doubts. He and Genie were enough, enclosed in their own perfect circle of love. She'd persisted, asking him to try it just once and saying that if he didn't like the experience, she would be content with one child.

He hadn't been overjoyed seeing her go through labor. Now, though he might feel inadequate as a father, he knew that with her love and support, he'd make it through, just as he'd made it through the previous years.

It wasn't hard to love when love was given so freely.

A slight movement on the bed caught his eye, and he turned his head. Christopher Mark Stanton was lying quietly on his tummy, his bottom in the air. His eyes were wide open and he seemed to be inspecting his new surroundings.

Remembering what the nurse had taught him in the child-care class, he gently eased his hands underneath the baby, supporting his head. Thinking Chris might be cold with only a diaper and a wrist bracelet on, Pierce placed him on top of one of the squares of flannel at the foot of the bed, then wrapped the blanket securely around the tiny body. Picking up his son, he placed him carefully against his chest.

It must have been the sound of his heartbeat that soothed Chris. The baby closed his eyes and relaxed, and Pierce stared down at the top of his head.

Though he knew he and Genie had reason to be prejudiced, even the nurses had agreed Chris was beautiful. Dark hair, blue eyes, pink skin. Perfectly formed fingers and toes. And he screamed like a banshee.

Pierce patted the baby's back gently, touching him with light circular soothing strokes. Having a child brought so many memories back. Some of them were good. He remembered more about his mother than he ever had before.

Be a little man. As he looked down on his son, he made a silent promise to himself. He would protect Chris with his life, never subject him to the hurts that had made up so much of his childhood. Chris had been wanted, would be surrounded by love his entire life.

As if in answer, the baby opened his eyes. Amazed

at the softness of his feelings, Pierce reached down and touched the small hand. Tiny fingers curled around one of his, and he was astounded by the strength of the infant's grip.

He felt a hand on his shoulder and looked over to see Genie watching him.

"So what do you think?" she whispered. "Isn't he the most beautiful thing you ever saw?"

He nodded, suddenly unable to speak.

"Are you mad that I talked you into it?"

He shook his head.

"Do you want to have another one?"

He nodded and found his voice. "Next time a girl. Just like you."

She seemed content and lay back among the pillows, wincing slightly.

"Sore?"

"You would be, too, if you'd just given birth to a football."

Chris started to whimper and Genie smiled. "I wasn't making fun of you, pumpkin. Come here, I'll feed you."

As she unbuttoned the top of her nightgown, Pierce brushed his finger against the baby's cheek. His head moved, mouth seeking.

"He's a feisty one," Genie said as she put Chris to her breast, supporting his head with her hand.

"Just like his mother," Pierce said softly. She'd never looked more beautiful to him, her hair falling softly below her shoulders, her hands gentle as she redirected Chris's exploring mouth.

"Whoa!" She flinched as the baby found her, starting to nurse.

"Does it hurt?" he asked.

"Only when I laugh," she replied, then reached out with her free hand, lacing her fingers between his. "You're sure you're okay?"

He put his arm around her shoulders, eased her back against his chest. "I'm fine. I called your sister this morning."

"Oh?" Genie raised an eyebrow. He'd never gotten along with Valerie since their argument at that party so long ago.

"I was feeling pretty good," he admitted.

"After what we went through?"

"I called her up to thank her. Because in her own crazy way, Val brought you into my life."

"Did she even understand what you were trying to say?"

"I don't think so," he admitted.

"I do," she whispered.

He kissed her then, his arm around her shoulders, his other hand helping her support the baby. He'd finally done away with all the masks, the endless defenses. The woman in his arms had helped him create a perfect circle of love, ever widening, ever expanding.

The best was yet to come. He was sure of it.